Tim Witkinson's life is really, really boring – until he turns into . . .

. . . daredevil
hero, Captain
Goodygoody . . .

. . . and
amazingly
clever Doctor
Intensive-Care.

But what's all this got to
do with chickens?

Jeremy Strong once worked in a bakery, putting the jam into three thousand doughnuts every night. Now he puts the jam in stories instead, which he finds much more exciting. At the age of three, he fell out of a first-floor bedroom window and landed on his head. His mother says that this damaged him for the rest of his life and refuses to take any responsibility. He loves writing stories because he says it is 'the only time you alone have complete control and can make anything happen'. His ambition is to make you laugh (or at least snuffle). Jeremy Strong lives near Bath with four cats and a flying cow.

Are you feeling silly enough to read more?

MY DAD'S GOT AN ALLIGATOR!
MY GRANNY'S GREAT ESCAPE
MY MUM'S GOING TO EXPLODE!
MY BROTHER'S FAMOUS BOTTOM

THE HUNDRED-MILE-AN-HOUR DOG
RETURN OF THE HUNDRED-MILE-AN-HOUR DOG
WANTED! THE HUNDRED-MILE-AN-HOUR DOG

BEWARE! KILLER TOMATOES
CHICKEN SCHOOL
KRAZY KOW SAVES THE WORLD – WELL, ALMOST

LAUGH YOUR SOCKS OFF WITH

Jeremy STRONG

Chicken School

Illustrated by

Rowan Clifford

PUFFIN

PUFFIN BOOKS

Published by the Penguin Group
Penguin Books Ltd, 80 Strand, London WC2R 0RL, England
Penguin Group (USA) Inc., 375 Hudson Street, New York, New York 10014, USA
Penguin Group (Canada), 90 Eglinton Avenue East, Suite 700, Toronto, Ontario, Canada M4P 2Y3
(a division of Pearson Penguin Canada Inc.)
Penguin Ireland, 25 St Stephen's Green, Dublin 2, Ireland (a division of Penguin Books Ltd)
Penguin Group (Australia), 250 Camberwell Road, Camberwell, Victoria 3124, Australia
(a division of Pearson Australia Group Pty Ltd)
Penguin Books India Pvt Ltd, 11 Community Centre, Panchsheel Park, New Delhi – 110 017, India
Penguin Group (NZ), 67 Apollo Drive, Mairangi Bay, Auckland 1310, New Zealand
(a division of Pearson New Zealand Ltd)
Penguin Books (South Africa) (Pty) Ltd, 24 Sturdee Avenue, Rosebank, Johannesburg 2196, South Africa

Penguin Books Ltd, Registered Offices: 80 Strand, London WC2R 0RL, England

penguin.com

First published 2004
This edition published 2007

6

Text copyright © Jeremy Strong, 2004
Illustrations copyright © Rowan Clifford, 2004
All rights reserved

The moral right of the author and illustrator has been asserted

Set in Baskerville MT
Made and printed in England by Clays Ltd, St Ives plc

British Library Cataloguing in Publication Data
A CIP catalogue record for this book is available from the British Library

ISBN 978-0-14-132240-7

This story is dedicated to all those Mrs Doves who rescue children, and in particular to the woman and the girl who saved me from my school and myself – Fanny Kennard and my wife, Susan.

Contents

1 Introducing . . .

And the winner of the Most Boring Family in the World award is . . . wait for it . . .

THE WITKINSONS OF WIDDLINGWALL!!!

Coming up on to the stage now we have Mr Thomas Witkinson, father of one, and current holder of the title, 'Most Uninteresting Father in Britain'. Mr Witkinson is forty-one and married to his wife – who else, ha ha ha! – married to his wife, Rachel.

Rachel, thirty-seven, is the proud champion of the My Hobby Is More Boring Than Yours Competition, 2004.

And finally, coming on to the stage now is their son, Tim, known to all his schoolmates – not that he has any – as Waste of Space. Tim has absolutely nothing at all of interest to tell you.

*

So there you are. It's true. We are a boring family. Do you know what my dad does? He has such an exciting job. He works for the Food Standards Agency. See – I knew you'd be impressed. I said to him one day: 'Dad, what do you actually *do*?'

And he said: 'It depends on what day it is. Monday is usually a fish day. I look at fish and see if they're fit for eating or not. Then on Tuesdays I look at beef and see if that's fit for eating or not.'

'Oh. That sounds fascinating, Dad. What do you do if it isn't fit for eating?'

'I throw it away.'

'And what do you do if it is fit for eating?'

'I write a report that says, "This beef is fit for human consumption". It's not a very demanding job.'

'Dad, Gary Jarvis's father is a wrestler. He gets into a ring with another wrestler and they throw each other about and try to pull each other's legs off and grunt and scream a lot.'

'Really?'

'Yes. And Sophie Goodsole's dad makes jet skis and he has to test them.'

And what does my dad do when he gets home from his boring job? Does he go extreme ironing? I think not. Does he swim with sharks? Not likely.

My dad plays choo-choos. He does. He's got a train set and he gets it out every night, along with his friend, Mr Smith.

It's true. They have a massive layout upstairs in our house. The track starts from a little model station in Mum and Dad's bedroom, travels across the room, out through a hole Dad knocked in the wall, across the staircase, through another hole in the wall and into the spare bedroom, right the way across until it reaches another model station at the end of the line.

And that's not all. There is a telephone link between them. If you stand anywhere upstairs you can hear the other person quite clearly without the phone, but Dad says it wouldn't be right if they didn't do it like they do at real stations.

Almost every evening Mr Smith comes round to our house and plays trains with my dad. They go upstairs. Dad sets up one of the engines on the track. He rings up his friend and it goes something like this:

My dad: Hello? Hello? Calling
  Appleton Station. This is
  Snowberry Station calling
  Appleton . . .
Mr Smith: I'm here,
  Snowberry. Is there a
  train due?
My dad: The eight fifteen 4-8-2 is
  about to leave and should
  arrive shortly.
Mr Smith: Message received,
  Snowberry. Goodbye.
My dad: Goodbye, Appleton.

And that's about it. What an
exciting time they have. Every
night! They follow a
timetable. It's all written
out. First one train, then
another, then another. In
between they make each
other cups of tea and dip
biscuits in their mugs and
chat about steam locomotives
and so on. The trains trundle

from one room to another, crossing the staircase (or the Grand Canyon, as Dad likes to refer to it) and then they come back again. Excitement! Thrills! Adventure!

???????
I DON'T THINK SO.

Then there's my mum. She has an incredibly exciting job – she's a librarian! Sometimes when she comes in from work she's all a-flutter because something amazing has happened. 'You'll never guess what – Mrs Tuttle brought back her books and, do you know, there was a fly squashed inside one. She said, "I can't read this, it's got a dead fly inside." So she brought it back.'

Gosh.

Sometimes I don't know how I cope with the level of excitement in our house. But wait for it, I haven't told you what my mum does while Dad is upstairs being an engine driver. She sticks seashells on flowerpots. She does! I bet you thought nobody actually does that, not for real!

Well, meet my mum, champion shell-sticker.

The rooms in our house are floor-to-ceiling with things that have shells stuck on them. If it doesn't move, it's probably got shells stuck on it. The TV? Covered with them (apart from the screen, of course). The downstairs toilet? Oh yes, encrusted with shells. Mum would have put them on the *seat* if I hadn't stopped her. Imagine that! Ouch!

Mum keeps her shell supply in the back room downstairs. It's as if an entire tropical-shell beach has been bulldozed into that room. If you open the door, shells come cascading out across the floor. We even got a crab once, which is probably why the garden's full of gulls. They line up on the roof. They queue in the garden, hoping the shells have still got something edible inside.

Just think of the exciting conversations my mum must have when she goes to a party.

Hostess: And what do you do for excitement, Mrs Witkinson?

My mum: I get lots of shells and I stick them on
  things.
Hostess: Really? How fascinating. Just hold still
  for a moment while I pour this bucket of cold
  custard over your head.

I ask you! What am I to do? Do you see how
colourless my life is? It was all right when I was
little. I liked whopping shells all over pots with
my mum when I was five or six. I liked playing
trains with my dad when I was seven or eight.
But I'm eleven now. Where's the excitement?
Where's the fun?

WHERE'S MY LIFE?!

It's no better at school. I'm in Mrs Dove's class.
I like Mrs Dove, even though she's extremely
old and grey. She's OK and occasionally, if
there's time, she gives us great things to do.
Sometimes we're allowed to write a whole story
– not just bits – and I like that. Or she might
read us a book or tell us about something really
exciting from the past, like ancient Egyptians
pulling brains out of people's noses, or baddies

being stuck in the stocks and having mouldy tomatoes thrown at them.

It hardly ever happens though because usually there *isn't* enough time because we have to follow THE TIMETABLE.

The timetable was set up by our head teacher, Mr Dedman, and he insists that everyone follows it. We have fifteen minutes for multiplication tables, and half an hour for literacy activities, and twelve and a half minutes for playing, and one minute twenty seconds to go to the loo, and a whole hour for sport (because Mr Dedman likes sport) and three minutes for creative writing, and absolutely no time at all for thinking or dreaming or just living.

I don't think Mrs Dove likes it any more than we do, so every once in a while she squeezes out some extra time so we can do something we like. Even so, she has to post a guard at the door to keep an eye out for Mr Dedman because he snoops around, checking up.

I don't exactly fit in at school anyhow. I listen to the others in my class talking about what they did at the weekend and it's all about going on the dry ski slope or visiting a theme park and things like that. All I have to talk about is train sets and different kinds of seashell.

I do have one friend, and that's Pete Smith. We get on pretty well, largely because it's Pete's dad who plays trains with my dad. In other words we share the same problem. Pete usually comes to my house with his dad and we sit up in my bedroom and we try and outdo each other by imagining ourselves as different beings. It's the only way to escape from the fact that we're really deadly dull.

I'll give you an example. One of my favourites is a horrible, blubbery monster called **The Thing From Thingummy**. Don't laugh! Stop it. I can hear you sniggering and you shouldn't because **The Thing from Thingummy** is pretty awesome. I become all green and lumpy and fat, like some big blubber monster. My skin is bubbly all over with giant warts. I get a fat, bloated face with flubbery lips and sharp white teeth. My eyes go all poppy and I have no hair left, no hair at all. Instead, all over the top of my skull, there are little horns, about twenty or thirty of them – little blunt-ended horns, like upside-down ice-cream cones.

Then I go off and do things . . .

I stepped out and crashed through the locked door. One big blow from one big fist was all it took. SMASH! I was out! I headed downstairs, my feet making every step on the stairs squeak and squeal.

POW! I smashed through the door of the front room, where Mum and Dad were watching TV. They turned and stared at me in horror.

'Oh, my God!' yelled Dad. 'What is it? What kind of creature is this?'

'We're going to die!' screamed Mum. 'What do you want from us, Big Green Blubber Monster?'

I scowled hideously at them and curled my lips. 'I have come to obliterate all manner of shelly pot things and all kinds of puff-puff trainy things,' I bellowed. 'Get rid of these at once or you will feel the full force of my wrath, for I am The Thing from Thingummy and woe betide those who do not obey.'

Mum and Dad threw themselves at my feet. They clutched at my warty green ankles and pleaded with me, snivelling like little babies who've just had their lollies taken away.

'No, no! We will do anything but that! Please let us play with choo-choos and shelly pots!'

'No! Never!' I roared. 'You must forsake such things and become Interesting and Exciting Parents! Do this and I shall be well pleased and leave you in peace.'

Mum and Dad moaned and groaned and eventually agreed to be interesting for the rest of their lives. I pounded back upstairs . . .

. . . and lo and behold! I'm me again – Tim Witkinson.

So that's what Pete and I play at to stop ourselves from dying of boredom.

Then one morning we went to school and my

life changed, because there, on the school wall, in big Day-Glo green spray-paint, was a message:

tim Witkinson
loves
Sophie Goodsole

2 A Visit to Mr Dedman

Of course I like Sophie. Who wouldn't? She sparkles. She's not only beautiful but she's funny too. We laugh about the same things and we've got so much to share. She's the kind of person you really want to know and be friends with, and that's half the trouble. Most of the boys in the class like her and, knowing my luck, I'm probably last in the queue as far as Sophie's concerned. I'd like to tell her how I feel but there's something else about me that I haven't told you yet.

I'm a mouse.

Not a real mouse, obviously. You know what I mean. I said before that I've only got one friend but that's only part of the story. The truth is, I find it really hard to make friends. It just seems to be the way I am. I find it difficult talking to people. I don't know what to say, and if I do it's probably something like: 'If an elephant stood at the edge of an ocean with its trunk in the water and made noises, would a whale understand what it was saying?'

And when I DO say things like that, they look at me with their faces all screwed up and they say: 'What kind of rubbish is that?' Then they wander off, leaving me standing there on my own (again) and the thing is – I REALLY WANT TO KNOW. Can the whale hear the elephant?

About the only person who does talk to me is Pete. He's a bit weedy, but then so am I. We both like Sophie and neither of us has told her. She's always laughing and smiling and she's got this long hair that's like sunshine, and green eyes and little freckles across her nose. She's brilliant at running, and gym, and netball, and that kind of stuff – all the sorts of things that Pete and I are hopeless at. She's clever too. She's always getting good reports. The only thing Mrs Dove ever says about me is: 'He's a quiet child.'

Anyhow, you can see why I have never said anything to Sophie. She wouldn't look twice at someone like me, but all I want is for her to notice me. It would be a start.

So there we were on that fateful morning when the Day-Glo writing appeared on the playground wall. The first thing that happened was that I was called to the head teacher's office.

Mr Dedman is small, thin and scrawny. He does all the sport at school. He doesn't actually *do* any sport himself. He watches, and what he likes most is when we are all in lines and he gets us doing exercises. 'Touch toes, stretch, jump, touch toes, stretch, jump,' and so on. I think he just loves bossing everyone about and watching them all do the same thing at the same time.

At weekends he goes off with his mates and races his Porsche on circuits. He's sport mad and he doesn't like me because I'm hopeless at all of them. I can't help it.

Sometimes I think my brain must be wired up all wrong because my arms behave like they think they're my legs, and my legs try to do what my arms should. It's like, you know, I'm out on the football pitch and the ball is coming towards me and my brain's thinking: 'Panic stations! Football approaching! Kick the ball! Kick the ball! Is that a leg? No, that's your arm, dimwit. Kick the ball with your foot! That's your knee! Don't knee the ball, kick it with your foot! Oh great, now you've fallen over. You're useless.'

Anyhow, I can think of better things to do with my time.

Mr Dedman was sitting behind his massive desk, drumming his fingers on the surface and drilling through my head with his beady little eyes. All at once he began bombarding me with questions.

'Witkinson, your name has come to my attention – come to everyone's attention, in fact. There it is on the school wall, in big letters. What made you do it? Why have you defaced school property? Have you considered how Sophie Goodsole might feel about this? Have you got any sense at all? Aren't you ashamed?'

'It wasn't me,' I said.

Mr Dedman looked incredulous. 'It's your name,' he snorted.

'That doesn't mean it was me. Anyone could have done it.'

'Why would someone else want to put *your* name up on the wall?'

'I don't know. I didn't do it. I'm hardly likely to, am I?'

'Why ever not?'

'It's obvious, isn't it? It's like a robber goes into a bank, steals the money and then writes his name on the wall, saying: "*Joe Bloggs did this. I live at 32 Laburnum Avenue. I'll be in after three, when I've finished spending all the money I've just stolen, or you can ring me on my mobile. The number is . . .*"'

'Stop it!' snapped Mr Dedman. 'What on earth are you going on about? Who's Joe Bloggs?'

'The robber who stole the money from the bank.'

'What bank?'

I shrugged. Did it matter? 'I don't know,' I said. 'Any bank, I suppose. I'm just trying to tell you I didn't write that sign on the wall.'

'But what about the bank robber?'

'There wasn't any robber,' I explained patiently.

'You said there was. I thought that was why you couldn't have written on the wall. I thought you meant the robber had done it.'

I searched Mr Dedman's face for some sign of brain activity. He stared back at me while I thought carefully about what I should say next. He was obviously a confused man. I decided to keep quiet and say nothing. Mr Dedman began drumming his fingers again. His eyes narrowed to slits.

'If it wasn't you, then it must have been Sophie Goodsole. Go and fetch her.'

I trailed all the way back to class. Of course Sophie hadn't done it. That was ridiculous. I knew just how she would react too – she'd want me dead. But there was no escape. I delivered Mr Dedman's message to Mrs Dove and even she raised her eyebrows.

She called Sophie out
and the poor girl
turned extremely red
and gave me the sort of
look that would kill an
elephant. (Good thing
I'm not an elephant –
ha ha.) As we walked
through the hall
towards Mr Dedman's

office I could almost feel her seething with fury.

'It's not my fault,' I muttered.

'It's your name! And mine!' she hissed back.
'It is *so* embarrassing!'

'I *didn't* do it.'

'Well, somebody did.'

'It wasn't me, Sophie.'

'And it wasn't me!' she snapped.

We reached the head's office. Mr Dedman
was still drumming away, but he stopped as we
walked in. He fixed his eyes on Sophie and
came straight out with it.

'Why did you do it, Sophie? You're captain of
the netball team!'

I ask you. Hadn't he learned anything? I had only just explained to him why it was so unlikely to be either me or Sophie. And what did being captain of the netball team have to do with it? Sophie didn't answer; she burst into tears.

I couldn't bear it. I wanted to put my arm round her shoulders and protect her. I wanted to whip out my laser-phaser and shout, 'Get back, sucker! Don't come any closer or I shall blast you into a squillion atoms with no chance of reassembly!' But of course I didn't. I stood there like a lemon, useless as usual.

Mr Dedman pushed a box of tissues across his desk. 'All right, all right, perhaps you didn't do it, but maybe you know who did?'

Sophie sniffed and shook her head. Mr Dedman gave me a further scowl and sighed heavily. 'All right, you two, go back to class. We appear to have a phantom scribbler at large in the school, but don't think the culprit is going to get away with this. I'll find out who it is, if it's the last thing I do, and they are going to pay for it.'

He eyeballed me yet again and nodded angrily. He obviously thought I was some kind of master criminal. I wanted to take him to one side and point out that my father played with trains and my mother turned waste-paper bins into shell-shocked bogey baskets, so I was hardly master-criminal material.

However, being a mouse, I slunk out into the corridor with Sophie and we trooped back to the classroom in silence. (I should say *almost* silence, because Sophie was still sniffing quietly.)

Now, I thought things had been pretty bad so far, but at playtime things got far worse. Hardly had I set foot outside when a two-legged rhino- ceros with bad breath and crooked teeth grabbed me by the throat and thrust me up against  the wall. I found myself staring into the fizzingly furious eyes of Juggernaut, more politely known as Gary Jarvis.

Gary is the sort of person you try to avoid at all costs. If you couldn't avoid him, then you tried to be his friend. Whatever you did, you made sure you stayed on the right side of Gary. That way you might possibly STAY ALIVE.

But today I was obviously on the wrong side and I could see Death approaching very, very quickly. Gary pressed his face up so close I could feel the spit from his mouth spatter my face.

'Keep clear of Sophie or you're going to look like mashed potato,' he squeaked. (Gary might have a body like a rhinoceros but his voice is more like a guinea pig's.) 'Got it?'

'Got it,' I croaked.

'Sophie Goodsole is mine,' he added, talking about her as if he'd just bought her at the supermarket.

'Does she know?' I couldn't help asking, and instantly felt myself being pushed even deeper into the wall. If this went on much longer, I would end up back inside my own classroom.

'Sophie and me are meant for each other,' he went on. 'So you – you keep clear!'

Juggernaut gave one last shove and dropped me to the ground. As he turned away I caught sight of Sophie. She had seen everything, probably heard everything too. She walked slowly towards me and my heart began to do stupid things, like going BANG BANG BANG. My brain was taking in all the things she might be going to say, like:

'Oh Tim, did Juggernaut hurt you? Are you all right? Can I kiss you better?'

Oh yes, Sophie, you certainly can!

But she didn't say all that. Instead she just hissed at me. 'Thanks a bundle.'

I was staggered. 'What have I done now?'

'Juggernaut only reckons I'm going to be his girlfriend.'

'Is that my fault?'

'It wouldn't have happened if that stupid heart and arrow hadn't appeared, would it?'

'No, I mean yes, no, I don't know! But it's not my fault.'

Sophie scowled back. 'Just stay out of my life, will you?' It was extraordinary how beautiful she looked even when she scowled. Then she was gone. Sophie hated me and my love life was in tatters. (No change there, then.)

Pete, who had been waiting some way off, well out of Gary's range, now decided it was safe to come over. He was all agog.

'What did she say?'

'To stay out of her life. Juggernaut Jarvis reckons she's for him only.'

Pete's face dropped. 'Bummer,' he muttered. We both watched as Gary swung his way back across the playground. Pete grunted and then added, ever so helpfully, 'You've got to watch Gary. He's trouble.'

3 Hurrah for Captain Goodygoody!

I raised my nose and sniffed the air. I sniffed to the right. I sniffed to the left. Aha! Something was amiss. I knew it! I am not Captain Goodygoody for nothing! No way. After all I am the daredevil hero: Tall, Dark, Handsome and Thoroughly Good. (Well, maybe not that tall because I'm only eleven, but I'm still growing.)

I am definitely Good, though. I am forever rescuing small children, puppies and kittens. I help frogs cross the road. However, this was something much bigger and far worse. My supersonic-tronic ears were picking up a distant distress call.

'Help!' it went, and then again, 'Help!' (It was very distant.) I had to strain my ears. 'Save me!'

A chill ran through my bones. That was the voice of Sophie Goodsole, the girl I loved! She was in grave danger, and I was pretty sure I knew who was behind it all.

I threw myself into the Goodykart, my super-ultra-mega-hypermobile, which travels at Dark Speed. I,

Captain Goodygoody, am the only person in the universe who knows the secret of Dark Speed, which is the exact opposite of light speed. At light speed you travel so fast you overtake everything. If you use Dark Speed you travel so slowly everything catches you up, and that way you can always get to where you want to go, or to be more precise, everywhere you want to go gets to you before you got there. That's clear then.

I tied my shoelaces extra tight, fired the retro-boosters, fastened my seat belt, pulled on my crash hat, popped a Cool-Breath mint into my mouth (the mint that gives you mint-fresh breath!) and took off.

Only a few minutes later I was circling a wild and remote island. It was a land full of high, jagged mountains, dark caves, night-filled forests and lurking beasties. It was a land where brambles shredded the skin from your bones and quicksands waited to suck you beneath their bubbles. It was a land that could be home to only one man – the fiendishly evil and desperately ugly Juggernaut Jarvis.

What had Juggernaut Jarvis done this time? He had kidnapped the wildly wilful and boldly beautiful Sophie Goodsole – my own secret love! Juggernaut Jarvis had carried her off to his island, where he intended to make her Mrs Juggernaut.

Oh no!

Oh yes!

Oh no!

(etc., etc., etc.)

I let the Goodykart silently descend through the purple cloud layer that drifted across the island. Juggernaut Jarvis would surely be expecting me and I was keeping a sharp watch. Just as well too, because suddenly, from out of nowhere . . .

Swoooooosh!

Swiiiiiish!

. . . two heat-seeking depleted uranium missiles came tearing towards the Goodykart. I threw the machine into a steep nosedive, spiralling down at breakneck speed and heading straight for the mouth of the island's growling volcano, already spewing lava as it prepared to swallow both myself and my speed machine. The missiles were still on my tail and gaining fast. I had a volcano in front and

missiles behind – gulp!

With the ground screaming up to meet me, I waited until the last moment before giving the rudder bar a sharp flip. The Goodykart went whizzing sideways, while the rockets plunged on down harmlessly into a lake of lava.

BADOOOOOMM!!

Phew! It had been a narrow escape, but I stayed cool and calm, because my underarm deodorant held fear at bay. (Do you smell of fear? Use Banish!! The only deodorant that banishes fear from your armpits.)

I quietly landed the craft and stepped out. Seizing my machete, I began to hack my way through the dense brambly undergrowth. Hardly had I managed three paces when I heard a spine-chilling roar from behind. Swiftly I turned, only to come face to face with . . .

. . . a nasty, skinny, stringy beastie. It was none other than the Gap-Toothed Deadbag.

What a foul and loathsome creature he was. He leapt about like a dancing maniac, drooling at the mouth, his tongue rolling, his hot eyes burning my skin. His fingers were like talons, his long nails like scythes. I prepared for his onslaught. I knew the Deadbag was capable of a tremendous bound. He would surely try to land on my shoulders, wrench off my head and kick it in the air like a football.

No matter, I had a trick or two up my sleeve as well, except that . . . oh no! I WAS WEARING A SHORT-SLEEVED SHIRT! I'd left all my tricks at home! Now I really would have to outwit the nasty beast.

The Deadbag ground his feet into the dust, grunting viciously to himself. 'Touch toes, stretch . . .' he began, and I knew for certain he was preparing to jump. What could I do?

There was only one thing for it. I ran away, very fast. Ha! That fooled him. He wanted to do jumping, but I did running away instead and left him fuming on the spot.

I followed the sound of those cries of distress: 'Help!' and then again, 'Help!' I was getting closer all the time, and at last I saw them both.

Sophie was tied to a tree, and Juggernaut Jarvis was stomping round her, shouting, 'You will marry me! It's no use struggling. You shall not be released until I have made you Mrs Juggernaut and I shall be your Lord and Master!'

'I shall never marry you, you hideously ugly old troll!' Sophie bravely returned. 'For I shall only marry the man I truly love, Captain Goodygoody!'

'Urgh! Yuck!' spat Juggernaut. 'Not that wimpy pimply do-gooder? Oh no, you will marry me and you will do it now, or I shall leave you tied to this tree all night, and all the horribly small nocturnal nibblers will come out and nibble you with their little jaws and tiny teeth, nibble nibble, until there's nothing left of you, not one single atom. You'll be nibbled to bits.'

'You fiend!' I yelled, leaping out into the open, no longer able to control my anger.

'Captain Goodygoody!' cried Sophie, blushing deeply. 'You've come to save me from the nibbly things!'

'Indeed I have. Fear not, Miss Sophie, for you shall soon be free.'

'Oh give us a break, wimpy-pimply,' sighed Juggernaut Jarvis. 'I am going to turn you into history and geography. First I shall kill you and then I shall scatter your bits far and wide.'

So saying, the monster seized a massive bazooka and pointed it directly at my chest.

He fired. Bamm! But I had used my hair-trigger responses to anticipate him – I ducked and the shell whizzed harmlessly over my head. Juggernaut snarled, threw the bazooka to one side and closed in. He wrapped his immense arms round me and began to squeeze and squeeze and squeeze, until I felt like a tube of toothpaste in the hands of a giant python. (Jolly good thing pythons don't have hands, eh?)

I managed to get my arms free of his grasp and I stuffed my fingers into his ears, as far as they would go. Then I shouted at him. '*** ** ****. * ***'* *******.'

'What?' he shouted back.
'*** ** ****!'

'What?' he shouted again. He stopped squeezing and put me down so that he could pull my fingers out of his ears.

'What did you say?' he repeated.

'I said: "Put me down. I can't breathe." And you have put me down. Thank you. Now I am afraid I shall have to do this!'

I drew myself up, twirled round three times on one foot, and delivered a massive King Kong Chip Chop, which is a very special martial art that nobody has ever heard of, not even me. (What a surprise I gave myself!) Juggernaut Jarvis fell to the ground in a heap, silent and still.

'Oh Captain Goodygoody!' cried Sophie, still struggling against the tree. I ran across and freed her from the ropes that bound her. For a short second she just looked at me gratefully, then, unable to stop herself, threw her arms round my neck and kissed me.

'Oh,' sighed Sophie. 'You have such lovely minty breath, Captain Goodygoody.'
Thank heavens for Cool-Breath mints, I thought.

And then I woke up.

4 A School Full of Chickens

Actually, no I didn't, because I wasn't asleep.
Sometimes I think that maybe I'm turning into
something like a shapeshifter. You've seen those
films on TV, where humans change into animals,
or aliens, or just about anything? You've seen
how their human shapes just sort of melt and
become something quite different?

That's what has been happening to me! I think
maybe I've been doing too much pretending
with Pete, because I find it happening without
thinking, at all sorts of odd moments. It seems so
real that I get lost in it.

At first I was worried because I felt like I
wasn't in control of myself. I went and stood in
front of the mirror in my bedroom and examined my face carefully, but all I could see was
Tim Witkinson in his pyjamas. Me being me.

Eventually I plucked up enough courage to ask
Pete about it on the way to school one morning.

'Does it happen to you as well?'

'Don't be daft.'

'Do you think I'm going crazy?'

'No.' Pete shook his head seriously and I felt a wave of relief. Then he added: 'You're not *going* crazy, Tim. You've always been crazy. I reckon all those trains have mashed your brain cells into little bits that don't work properly any more.'

'Thank you,' I nodded. 'Is that your professional opinion as a world-class brain surgeon?'

'It is indeed,' grinned Pete. 'Keep taking the tablets.'

By this time we had reached school and immediately spotted the excited huddle of people at the far end of the playground. Everyone was buzzing with curiosity and there was quite a lot of chuckling going on too. It seemed that The Phantom Scribbler had struck again.

We pushed our way to the front and stared at the Day-Glo green message.

This building is
full of chickens

'What's that supposed to mean?' asked Pete.

I shrugged.

'Prrarrrrkkkk, prrarrrkkkk,' went Gary Jarvis. 'I'm a chicken! Hey, everyone, look! Prrarrrkkk!'

'Jarvis! Is this your doing?' It was Mr Dedman.

'No way!'

The head teacher eyeballed Gary for several seconds and then his stare suddenly focused on each of us in turn. He lowered his voice to a sinister growl. 'So, what do you know about chickens, eh? Is there something funny about chickens and this school? Have any of you *seen* a chicken, maybe? Harry Franklin – what do you know about chickens?'

'They're farm birds, sir. They lay eggs.'

'Don't be smart with me, Franklin. You know what I mean.'

But Harry didn't know what Mr Dedman meant. None of us knew what he meant, except possibly Summer Frost. (Honest! That really is her name!)

'I think it means we're the chickens,' said Summer. 'You know, a bit brainless . . .'

'Ah, brainless,' smiled Mr Dedman. 'That would certainly be right.'

' . . . and because we're kept cooped up in class and we all have to do the same thing all the time and we're not allowed to think for ourselves.'

Mr Dedman took a threatening step towards her. 'You couldn't think for yourself even if you had a brain, Summer. Besides which, I do not like what you are suggesting.' He straightened up. 'Do I take it that none of you has the courage to own up to this bit of vandalism?'

'Who'd be that daft?' Gary answered, a big grin on his face.

Now Gary was either being very brave to

speak out like this, or he was rather stupid. Send your answer to . . . no, come to think of it, don't bother. It's too obvious and, needless to say, Mr Dedman was not impressed.

'There is something going on here,' he growled. 'It seems to me that this whole class is in it together. Gary, what exactly do you know?'

'Know about what, sir?'

'Chickens, this school, and this nasty scribble on the wall.'

'Nothing. I don't know nothing.'

Mr Dedman's hand descended on Gary's shoulder. 'I think you'd better come to my office.'

'But I didn't do it!'

'So you keep saying,' said Mr Dedman. 'To my office, Jarvis – now.'

We all breathed a sigh of relief once they'd gone and, of course, immediately got back to discussing who might really have done it. We knew it couldn't have been Gary. For a start he probably couldn't spell chicken properly.

Mrs Dove came across from the staff room. She stopped at the message, read it through a few times, and sighed. But there was something

weird. Even though she looked as if she was saddened by the whole business, there was a kind of secrecy about her, as if she was hiding something, as if she had a hidden face underneath her real face. I was sure I could see an invisible smile hovering around her mouth, which wasn't smiling at all.

Mrs Dove called us into class and went through the register. 'Sophie – ah yes, her mother rang, she's not well.'

A chorus of sighs came from various boys in the class, including Pete and me. Mrs Dove raised her eyebrows. 'Yes, boys, I am sure you are all very disappointed. Sophie has suspected German measles and will be off for the rest of this week, and the next, I shouldn't wonder. Now let's move on.

'The Phantom Scribbler has struck again and the feeling amongst the teaching staff is that the most likely suspects are, sadly, in this very class, because you are the oldest in the school. It is unlikely that younger children would get up to a trick like this.

'It pains me to think that one of you – some-one in *my* class – might be responsible. If any of you have anything to tell me, then you know where I am, and I might add that anything you do tell me will be between you and me only. It is not too late to stop what is happening and forget all about it. However, if it carries on, then it will be very difficult for me to be of help to any of you, and the matter will almost certainly be in the hands of Mr Dedman.' Mrs Dove paused to let the message sink in. 'Do you all understand what I am saying?'

Too right we did! I thought that was pretty cool of Mrs Dove and I don't suppose Mr Dedman would have been very pleased to hear it. However, there was something far more important bothering me.

Sophie was ill. Measles. German measles! Not ordinary measles, but German ones!

'Mrs Dove?'

'Yes, Tim?'

'Can you get Spanish measles?'

'No, Tim.'

'Arctic measles?'

Mrs Dove sighed. The whole class sighed.

'No, Tim. They're always German measles.'

'Why do they come from Germany, and how do they get here? I mean, do you think they come in a lorry? Do they come by plane? Do you get loads of measles waiting at German airports to catch planes to England? Why do they come here anyhow?'

'Tim, you're being silly.' Mrs Dove was beginning to laugh, but at that moment the door banged and in came Gary, back from Mr Dedman's office. He slammed the door behind him, marched across to his table, threw himself into his chair and grunted loudly. Mrs Dove raised her eyebrows.

'Anything wrong, Gary?'

'He only thinks I did it! Reckons I've got a thing about chickens.'

'It does seem likely that whoever has been painting these messages comes from an older class,' Mrs Dove repeated.

'Don't know why you're telling me,' growled Juggernaut. Mrs Dove slowly shook her head.

'No,' she murmured.' Neither do I, Gary. All right, everyone, let's get down to work. You have seventeen minutes for today's spellings, thirty-six minutes to do pages eight and nine in your maths text book, questions five to fourteen. Mr Dedman says that when you have finished, you can have two minutes to write a poem.'

'A whole poem? Two minutes?' asked Harry Franklin. 'Can we choose our own subject?'

'I'm afraid not,' answered Mrs Dove. 'You know Mr Dedman always likes to choose the subject. The title is "Wednesday".'

'Wednesday'. What a brilliant title – and a whole two minutes to write about it too, *if* you could possibly think of anything to say about 'Wednesday'.

And so class work began, another exciting day of timetabled exercises. I couldn't concentrate, not while Sophie was at Death's Door with deadly dangerous measles. Wasn't measles one of those illnesses with complications? Sophie could be in deeply serious trouble.

5 Hurrah for Doctor Intensive-Care!

'Get the crash team! Emergency! Emergency!'

*The nurses rushed the trolley down the long hospital
corridor, wheels spinning and clattering on the hard floor.
A young girl was bouncing about on board, more dead
than alive. Most of her face was obscured by an oxygen
mask. Clustered around vertical rods were several drip
bags, feeding different-coloured fluids through long tubes
into her arms: a red one, a yellow one, and a blue one.*

*'Where's the surgeon?' demanded Nurse Pillbox, as the
team skidded round a corner on two wheels, scattering
patients and staff in all directions.*

*'I'm here,' snarled Doctor Dedinbed, and the three
nurses groaned inwardly. Dedinbed's nickname amongst
the staff was 'The Butcher'. Now he trotted alongside,
taking the patient's pulse and giving directions. 'This
way,' he ordered.*

*A moment later they burst through the double plastic
doors and found themselves skittering across the car park,
with the trolley crashing against the sides of cars. The*

girl on the trolley had turned a funny colour.

'You must have taken a wrong turning outside the
X-ray Department, you useless lot,' yelled Doctor
Dedinbed. 'Swing round and head back to Casualty.'

'She's gone hyper-indigo,' warned Nurse Swab.

'What?' asked Dedinbed, completely nonplussed.

'She's turned blue,' explained Swab. 'It's OK, under
control, disconnect Blue Stuff and switch to Red Stuff.'

'Got it,' snapped Nurse Fingerstall. 'Red Stuff coming
on-line now.'

The trolley crashed back into the main hospital building

and screeched to a halt at a crossroads where four long corridors went off in different directions.

'Which way?' shouted Doctor Dedinbed. Pillbox and Swab eyed each other and shrugged. Nurse Fingerstall pulled an A-to-Z map of the hospital from her pocket and they stood in a huddle, poring over the directions.

'I knew we should have gone left at Maternity and straight on through Casualty,' muttered Fingerstall crossly.

'Surely there's a short cut through Amputations?'

'Only if you're on the second floor,' Swab pointed out.

At that moment the patient on the trolley began to convulse, legs and arms thrashing, the body making little jumps. 'She's having an exo-cardigan seizure,' observed Doctor Dedinbed.

'What does that mean?' chorused the nurses.

'She'll die unless we get her into surgery within five minutes and counting, four minutes fifty-nine, four minutes fifty-eight, four minutes fifty-seven . . .'

'Go! Go!' yelled the nurses in alarm, and they set off once more for the operating theatre. Racing down the corridor, Fingerstall asked who the patient was.

'Sophie Goodsole,' answered the doctor. 'She was brought in with suspected German measles, but she had complications. It turned into coughalottitis, and now she has third-stage soonbeagonna.'

'Is there any hope?'

Doctor Dedinbed shook his head. 'There's little I can do for her.'

'Doctor Intensive-Care could save her,' suggested Nurse Fingerstall, blushing deeply.

'Doctor Intensive-Care?' snarled Dedinbed, his mouth twisting into a cruel sneer. 'Oh yes, of course, you must mean that young, handsome and amazingly clever surgeon who has saved thousands of people's lives already, even though he's only eleven and has never had any medical training?'

'Yes, that Doctor Intensive-Care.' Nurse Pillbox heaved a sigh of admiration. 'If only he were here. Things are looking grave for Sophie.'

'Indeed,' muttered Doctor Dedinbed. 'The grave is exactly where she's heading.'

'Not if I have anything to do with it!' I cried, leaping out into the corridor and bringing the trolley to a halt.

'Oh, Doctor Intensive-Care!' sighed the nurses, looking at me with such admiration that I was almost embarrassed. But I had to think of my patient.

Sophie had turned a deep violet colour, what with the mix of red and blue in her system.

'What's the problem?'

'It's Sophie, doctor,' sobbed Nurse Swab. 'She's going to die unless you can work some miracle with her. She's got third-stage soonbeagonna.'

I bent over the patient. Sophie! My own true love! And she was dying! Of death! I took her pulse. Normally it should have been around seventy beats a minute, but Sophie's was more like 365! I took her blood pressure. It was 238 over 190 – but what did that mean? If only I knew. Not for the first time I cursed my primary school education. If only we had done more hands-on surgery and less football. I made a snap decision.

'Get her into surgery, and fast. I'll scrub up.'

'Are you going to operate, doctor?' asked Nurse Pillbox, and I nodded. I quickly washed my hands, put on my gown, mask, gloves and wellington boots, and went to the operating table. Sophie was already there. She was dying fast and that meant that I would have to operate even faster.

'You're a fool, Intensive-Care,' hissed Dedinbed scornfully. 'Nobody has ever survived third-stage soonbeagonna.'

I ignored him and bent over the patient. 'I'm going to have to do an emergency appendecklyrecklyvenalrenalostomy. Let's open her up. Scalpel.'

Nurse Fingerstall stifled a cry of dismay. 'The instruments aren't here, doctor! They're still in the dishwasher. There's nothing to operate with. The patient is going to die!'

'Steady, nurse,' I answered calmly. 'Just pass me that knife and fork left over from lunch.'

'Oh, doctor! That is so clever! Would you like the spoon as well?'

'Good thinking, nurse. It may be needed. All right, everyone, let's see if we can save this poor girl.'

I made an incision. Blood welled up and I couldn't see where I was cutting. 'Straw,' I called.

Nurse Pillbox bent over the patient with a large drinking straw and sucked the blood out of the way. 'Hmmm, nice,' she murmured, dabbing at her lips.

'Pass me that spoon, nurse. Looks like we shall need it after all. Thank you.' I plunged in with the spoon and gave everything a good stir. In a few moments I had managed to remove the heart, lungs, liver and kidneys.

'Excellent. That gives us room to work. Nurse, put these on separate plates and label them so we don't forget which is which. It's important to be methodical.'

'Let me mop your fevered brow, doctor,' cooed Nurse Fingerstall.

'No, let me,' insisted Nurse Pillbox. 'I'm the senior nurse here.'

'Nurses!' snapped Doctor Dedinbed. 'Stop swooning over Doctor Intensive-Care and look after the patient.'

I threw Dedinbed an amused glance. 'Are you jealous, Dedinbed? I'm sorry if I'm so fantastic, but it's a natural talent and there's nothing I can do about it. Perhaps you'd like to take over this operation?'

'Damn you, Intensive-Care! You know I can't perform an appendecklyreckly-venalrenalostomy, and certainly not without anaesthetic. Just get on with it.'

Beep! Beep! Beep! Beep! One of the monitors went on red alert. 'She's hyper-charging, doctor,' warned Nurse Fingerstall. 'If she continues like this much longer, there's a danger her legs will fall off.'

'Will she ever be able to walk again?' wailed Nurse Swab, wringing her hands.

Doctor Dedinbed folded his arms across his chest.

'Well, well, well. What are you going to do now, Doctor Smartypants? The girl's going to lose her legs, and you know as well as I do that hyper-charging will fatally damage her liver.'

'Not so, Dedinbed. You forget that I have already removed her liver to prevent that very thing from happening.'

'Raargh! Double damn you! I have to admit that even though I hate you, you are an extraordinarily fine surgeon.'

'I accept your praise,' I nodded. 'Now, if you'll excuse me, I must save Sophie.'

The operation continued. I managed to stabilize Sophie's hyper-charging and consequently her legs didn't fall off. I arrested the third-stage soonbeagonna and replaced her heart, liver, lungs and kidneys.

'She's stabilizing,' murmured Nurse Pillbox, almost as if it was a miracle, which of course it was. Maybe I hadn't shown it, but I'd been worried.

'Heart and pulse normal,' reported Nurse Fingerstall. She glanced at me with her big doe eyes and whispered, 'Can I have your autograph?'

I straightened up and looked at the clock. Four minutes had passed since I had first picked up the knife and fork. It had been one of my longest operations ever, and I was exhausted. I turned to Dedinbed. 'Will you close for me, doctor?'

'It will be a privilege,' he said, for even though he hated my guts, he had to admit I was a brilliant surgeon. I stepped back and, while he found a needle and searched for some thread to match her skin colour, I gazed down at Sophie. Looking at her beautiful face, it was hard to believe that she had just been through a major operation, and that she had almost lost her life.

Her eyelids fluttered and suddenly opened. She gazed

directly at me. 'Doctor Intensive-Care,' she whispered, a tiny smile on her lips.

'Sophie,' I croaked.

'It was bad, wasn't it?'

'Touch and go,' I admitted.

'You saved my life.'

'Yes.'

'Thank you.' Her wonderful eyes rested their grateful gaze on mine. Doctor Dedinbed finished his stitching and the nurses began to push the trolley back to the ward, carefully following Fingerstall's A-to-Z. As she drifted past, Sophie lifted a pale hand to her lips, smiled and blew me a kiss.

6 And After the Chickens – a Rabbit

Well, it might happen. It could. Just because it hasn't doesn't mean it won't. The important thing is that I shall always be here to save Sophie's life, on guard against any peril that might threaten her. Anyhow, it was a great deal more interesting than life at home, as you yourselves are about to find out. Want to know about the latest instalment in the fascinating saga, 'At Home with the Witkinsons'? Let me tell you.

When I got home from school, Dad was standing in the kitchen with Mum, explaining something in great detail. He seemed to be quite excited, so as you might imagine my ears pricked up. I know you shouldn't listen to other people's conversations, especially grown-ups', but if you don't listen, you don't find out anything. (Which is why they don't want us to listen.)

'And then we take the new track out through the wall at a higher level and across the landing.'

'That means there'll be two railway lines to step over,' complained Mum.

'No, that's the beauty of it. The new track will pass above us – over our heads! It will be so high it will be like crossing the Forth Bridge, which is exactly what we're going to model the new line on.'

'The Forth Bridge? In our stairwell?'

'Yes! It will be stupendous. I can hardly wait to start!' Dad paused a moment and cleared his throat. 'You can come in, Tim. You don't have to stand out there trying to hear what we're saying.'

I shuffled into the kitchen, feeling not just embarrassed but cross. Why did I have to live in a house festooned with railway lines? 'So, when Tim and I walk upstairs we have to step over the old track and then duck under the new line?' Mum went on.

Dad scratched his head. 'I've already said it will be above your head. You won't have to duck.'

'How long will it take to build?' asked Mum.

'A couple of days for the simple bit, and then weeks to make it realistic. The knocking-through will only take a few hours.'

Mum nodded. 'Make sure it does. Anyhow, I've had an idea too. I've been getting a bit tired of sticking shells on flowerpots, and the other day I was in a craft shop and I saw some knitted covers for toilet rolls. They were ever so clever. They were dolls really, wearing big knitted dresses, and you stick the doll's legs down the toilet tube and spread the dress over the toilet roll.'

'Why would you want to do that?' asked Dad.

'So that you don't have to stare at the spare roll on the window ledge. Instead you can look at –'

'– a doll with a toilet roll stuck up her dress,' I said.

'Tim! That's not a nice way to put it.'

'I don't think it's nice sticking toilet rolls up –'

'That's enough,' snapped Mum. 'Anyway, I'm not going to make a doll for the toilet roll.'

'You're not?' asked Dad. 'What are you going to do?'

'It's really exciting! It's something completely different. I looked all round the shop, but they didn't have one.' Mum beamed at us both.

'Didn't have one what?' we chorused.

'A woolly jumper for a flip-top bin.'

Dad's eyebrows shot up his head and almost took off. Mine were already stuck to the ceiling. Woolly jumpers for swing bins?

'Yes. If you can have dresses for toilet rolls, why not jumpers for bins? I thought, that's a good idea. That's something new and different. They'll be like jumpers except they won't have sleeves, because swing bins don't have arms.'

'No, they don't,' I agreed, though I thought it

was an interesting idea – a swing bin with arms. Maybe it could be trained to open and shut its own lid. And if it could have arms, why not legs? A swing bin with legs, running round the kitchen in a stripy jumper, looking for rubbish.

'I expect there are loads of people who'd like to buy a woolly cover for their flip-top bin,' said Mum dreamily.

'Would you put buttons down the front like a cardigan, Mum, or have a V-neck?'

Mum didn't pick up on my tone at all. She was still in dreamland. 'Oh, it would have to be a jumper, or maybe a polo-neck sweater. That could be good.'

I crept away from this sad, sad scene and stumbled upstairs to my room where I threw myself on my bed in deep despair. The only glimmer of light that shone into my life was the fact that at least toy trains and woolly jumpers for swing bins would keep my parents off the streets, and that meant that nobody would ever know what strange, weird parents I had. If my friends at school ever found out, they would never, ever stop laughing.

I turned my attention to more important things, like the Phantom Scribbler. He (or she!) was certainly having quite an effect at school. Mr Dedman was about to erupt like a rhinoceros that had swallowed a volcano, and everyone was talking about it. The school had suddenly come alive and of course everyone (including me) was desperate to know just who the Phantom Scribbler was.

'I reckon it's Juggernaut,' said Pete.

'You only have to look at his face to see it's not him, Pete. Juggernaut hasn't got the brain to even think about such a thing, let alone do it.'

Pete screwed up his face. 'Is it my imagination or has Dedhead got chickens on the brain? He goes on and on about them. Why ask us if we'd seen chickens? I think he's going loopy.' Pete stared into space for a bit and suddenly straightened up. He looked at me with big, excited eyes.

'What about Harry Franklin?!'

'Yeah! That's possible, that is definitely a possibility. He does like playing jokes on people.'

'We should keep an eye on Harry,' suggested Pete.

'You mean keep a tail on him, like we're detectives?'

Pete nodded, and the more I thought about it the more I realized he could be on to something. Harry Franklin had always been the class joker, ever since the time he was in Year Three and he brought a whoopee cushion into school and put it on Mrs Chappell's chair. OK, so a whoopee cushion on the teacher's chair was not exactly an original idea, but attaching a microphone to it and connecting the microphone to the radio amplifier in the main hall was.

Mrs Chappell had a habit of sneaking out of Friday assembly and going to the classroom for a quiet sit-down at her desk. Everybody knew about it. So one Friday, off she went and sat down and **SPLLLLLLLLRGH!** Halfway through assembly there was this enormous farty noise and we all fell about. Most of the teachers fell about too, all except for Mrs Chappell, who came storming out of her room waving the whoopee cushion (making us double up all over again), and Mr Dedman, who couldn't see a joke even it was painted pink with green stripes and was the size of an elephant.

Yes, the culprit could certainly be Harry Franklin.

I have a kind of love–hate relationship with Harry, I suppose. I had a grudging admiration for him because he was an OK kind of person. He wasn't a friend – like I said, I only had one friend and that was Pete – but Harry wasn't an enemy either. He was easygoing and almost everyone in the class liked him, especially the girls, much to Juggernaut's annoyance.

So Pete and I decided to keep an eye on Harry. We followed him home for a few days. We kept watch outside his house for as long

as we could without getting into trouble ourselves. We even went back after dark and hid
near his house and watched. Pete took some
photographs.

'So we know what he looks like,' he explained.

'But we've been in the same class for years.
We *do* know what he looks like.'

'OK,' said Pete, getting all huffy. 'You describe
him to me.'

'Pete, he looks like Harry Franklin.'

'You're just jealous because you didn't think of
it.'

'No, I'm glad because I didn't think of it.
Only an idiot would think of it.'

'So I'm an idiot?'

'Yes.'

Pete and I spent several pleasant hours having
cheerful exchanges like that, and in the end the
only thing we learned was that Harry's mum
was a giant rabbit. One evening the family car
turned into the drive, stopped, and out stepped
a giant rabbit wearing a blue waistcoat and
carrying a handbag. I looked at Pete.

'Blimey, Pete, I thought my mum was odd,
knitting jumpers for swing bins, but Harry's

mum is a giant rabbit. The world's gone mad.'

'Do you think Harry knows?'

'He must do! You can't live with a giant rabbit and not notice.'

The next morning at school we told Harry we knew his mum was a rabbit. He turned ever so red and put on a massive scowl. 'I've asked her not to come home like that,' he muttered. We waited for an explanation but there was none, so Pete asked Harry if his dad was a rabbit too.

'Don't be stupid!' he grunted.

'If your mum's a rabbit, then why shouldn't your dad be one?'

'Because,' he went on, lowering his voice. 'I don't want anyone to know. Promise you won't tell? Mum was working in an office but she got made redundant and she's been looking for work for ages and the only thing she could get was –'

' – being a giant rabbit?' Pete filled in. Harry nodded and turned even redder. 'Why would anyone need a giant rabbit?'

'You two are useless,' snorted Harry. 'She's not any old rabbit. She's Peter Rabbit. You know, Flopsy, Wopsy, Sploppit and Doodah. *That* rabbit.'

'Ah!' Light began to dawn. Of course. We should have guessed, I suppose, although not knowing and wondering had been such fun. The answer to the mystery wasn't very interesting at all. It was funny though.

'I knew you'd laugh,' sulked Harry.

I patted him gently on the back. 'If it were my mum, or Pete's mum, *you'd* laugh, wouldn't you?'

'No! Maybe. Probably. But don't tell anyone.'

'Mum's the word,' said Pete, zipping his lips.

'Actually, I think rabbit's the word,' I smiled, although I was wishing that I could go home and discover that *my* mother was a giant rabbit – or, come to think of it, anything other than a sweater designer for flip-top bins.

So trailing Harry didn't get us any further and anyhow it wasn't long before the Phantom Scribbler struck again, and this time the message was rather odd. The lettering had been done quite neatly, so that it looked very much like a shop sign.

DEDMAN'S CHICKEN FACTORY

But that wasn't all. A bit further over was another heart with names in the centre.

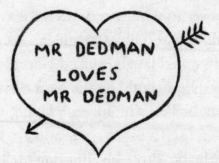

7 The Culprit Is Revealed

'What's that supposed to mean?' demanded
Gary, chewing gum and rolling it from one side
of his mouth to the other. A big bunch of us
stood in front of the wall, considering the latest
Day-Glo heart.

'That's mad,' muttered Vikram.

'He's a nutcase,' grunted Gary.

'Who? Dedman?'

'No, whoever wrote it.' Gary added crossly, 'It
doesn't make sense.'

'Of course it does,' said Pete and everyone
turned to look at him. He blushed a little.
'Dedman is interested in nobody but himself.
He thinks he's top guy – that sort of thing, and
it's true, isn't it?'

Gary poked Pete's chest with a thick, dirty finger.
'Proper little clever clogs, aren't you? Right little
psychia-wotsit. How come you know so much all
of a sudden? I reckon *you're* the one who wrote it.'

I have never seen Pete look so red. It happened in a flash. One moment his face had just a faint blush and the next, whooosh, he was Tomato Man. The group pressed in closer all around him, everyone talking at once.

'Did you? Did you, Pete?'

'Was that you?'

'Did you do the other an' all?'

'You never did! Did you?'

All at once Pete roared out at the top of his voice. 'IT WASN'T ME! LEAVE ME ALONE!' He pushed his way through the crowd, raced across the playground and vanished into the school building, leaving us staring after him.

Gary rubbed his hands with satisfaction. 'I think we touched a raw nerve there. Something tells me he's got something to hide.' Juggernaut was about to go loping after Pete, but he changed his mind suddenly. Coming through the school gates was a vision.

It was Sophie Goodsole, back at school. Gary flung a massive arm round her shoulders. 'Babe! You're better!'

Sophie winced and quickly lifted the arm

away from her. Gary grinned back at the rest
of us.

'My girlfriend,' he growled proudly.

'I am *not* your girlfriend,' snapped Sophie.

'She is really,' insisted Gary, still smiling. 'She
likes to pretend.'

'I am not pretending, Gary.' She tried to move
further away but he still clung to her. His face
had lost its smile.

'If I say you are, then you must be,' he insisted.

I couldn't stand any more of this nonsense. It
was bad enough being ordered around by
Dedhead, without having to put up with
Juggernaut as well. I stepped forward. I knew I
was probably going to die, but I had to say
something. 'Gary, you can't make other people
be whatever you want them to be.'

Juggernaut's eyes narrowed and I could
almost see the hair on his head start bristling.
'What's that supposed to mean?'

'Sophie has to decide for herself. You can't tell
her what to think.' I glanced at Sophie. She had
taken a few steps back and now she stared at the
ground, taking no notice. I suddenly realized
that all the other kids had distanced themselves

too, leaving Juggernaut and myself alone, like gladiators in a Roman arena. It was Tiny Tim versus The Rhinoceros.

Juggernaut pressed closer. 'Are you telling me what to do?'

I was going to say 'no', but the blow came out of the blue. He just threw a punch and I wasn't expecting it, which was pretty stupid of me, because that's what Juggernaut does – punches people. He'll probably still be doing it when he's thirty, forty, fifty. I could picture him on one of those TV quiz shows where the presenter says:

'And what do you do, Mr Juggernaut?'

'I punch people.' (Said with a smile and great pride, of course.)

So there I was on the ground, on my knees, struggling to breathe, while Juggernaut turned on his heels and walked off. The little crowd drifted away in the opposite direction, Sophie amongst them.

I was on my own again. I knelt there for a short while, until I got my breath back and was able to stand up. What a weird start to the day! It was only when school began that I discovered Sophie's measles had turned out to be a virus. Those German germs must have missed their plane.

Not surprisingly, Mr Dedman was furious about the new messages and got the caretaker to rub them out at once. He delivered a lecture about how we should all take pride in the school and stop that silly nonsense and all that kind of stuff.

We knew what he was going to say even before he opened the door. He could have stayed in his office and saved his breath.

However, we didn't expect him to put us in detention. 'All boys will remain behind after school until the culprit comes forward and owns up.' His weasel eyes fixed on Harry. 'Franklin, why is your hand up?'

'That's not fair, sir.'

'Oh? Not fair? Let me tell you something, laddie. I don't think it's fair to write all over the school walls. I don't think it's fair to leave rude messages where anyone can read them. That's what isn't fair!'

'But sir, why only the boys? One of the girls might have done it.'

'Don't be ridiculous. Girls wouldn't do anything like that.'

'I would, sir,' interrupted Summer, and she probably would too, even though it was not very bright of her to tell the head teacher.

'You would?'

'Yeah. It's women's rights.'

Mrs Dove appeared to have a choking fit in the corner of the classroom. She patted her chest and turned her face to the wall so I was unable to see her properly. The head scowled angrily at Summer, but in the end he had to admit that, yes, it might just as easily have been done by a girl.

'And since that might be the case, *everyone* from Year Six will be kept in after school.'

The girls groaned. 'Thanks a bunch, Summer,' they muttered.

'You've only yourselves to blame,' Mr Dedman said. 'Someone here knows something about chickens and I want to know who it is. If the culprit comes forward, it would save us all a lot of bother.'

After school had finished we all stayed at our desks in silence. At least we were supposed to sit in silence but there was a lot of whispering going on, most of it the angry pointing-the-finger kind, especially from Gary.

'Pete, admit it.'

But Pete kept his eyes on his book and wouldn't lift them, not even to look at me. There was definitely something bothering him, and that got me thinking.

What worried me was that Gary might be right. It could have been Pete. But then it could have been Gary, or Harry, or Summer, or indeed anyone in the class. In fact, come to think of it, it could be anyone in the whole school.

Anyone.

Adults included.

It could be Mrs Dove.

I studied her carefully. I had always liked her. She seemed warm and cuddly, but there was also something unexpected about her. You never quite knew what she was going to say or do. I had a strong suspicion that not only did she dislike Mr Dedman, but that he knew she didn't like him. She had no time for people who threw their weight around, people like Gary Jarvis and the head.

I realized I was smiling to myself, almost laughing. It was such a great thought: Mrs Dove as the Phantom Scribbler! I could picture her propping up a ladder by the school wall in the darkness, trying to scramble over and getting stuck with one leg either side of the wall. That would be the sort of daft thing that would happen to Mrs Dove.

I was deep into considering all these matters when Mr Dedman reappeared. He frowned at everyone and again demanded to know who was responsible for the graffiti. 'I'm bound to find out sooner or later,' he growled. 'Better to admit it now and get it over with.'

A chair at the back of the class scraped and every head turned to see who it was.

Sophie!
She was getting to her feet!
She was walking towards the front of the class!
Blimey!

Mr Dedman was totally gobsmacked. Even Mrs Dove looked surprised. Sophie wasn't the least bit fazed. She stood in front of the head teacher and said very calmly: 'It was me, Mr Dedman. I did it. Can everyone go home now?'

The head began to splutter. 'But, Sophie, I'm sure you didn't, you couldn't, why? I mean, you didn't . . .' He ran out of words.

'I did it,' Sophie repeated. Mr Dedman gazed helplessly across at Mrs Dove. She was wearing that hidden smile of hers again. Why? Why? What on earth was going on? Did Mrs Dove know something we didn't – something that not even Mr Dedman knew?

By this time the rest of us were packing our things and trailing out of the classroom. Nobody had said we could go, but nobody was stopping us either. As I left I glanced back across the hall. Through the open classroom door I could see Mr Dedman looking very puzzled. Sophie hadn't moved. She stood there, defiant, lost, beautiful.

8 Hurrah for James Blond!

I perched on the edge of Miss Pennyfarthing's desk, idly twisting a single white carnation between my fingers.

'James,' said Miss Pennyfarthing. 'Have you suddenly taken up flower arranging for when you're not whizzing round the globe catching spies and chasing supercriminals?'

'It's for you, Miss Pennyfarthing,' I smiled. 'A beautiful flower for a beautiful lady.' Z's secretary blushed. I have to admit that I am devilishly handsome, debonair, a crack shot and irresistible to women, but nevertheless, I only had one true love, and sadly it was not Miss Pennyfarthing.

'Oh James!' she blushed. 'You'd better go in and see the chief. He's expecting you.'

She pressed a button on her desk. The picture on the wall slid up into the ceiling. The wall slid down into the floor, revealing a door. An infra-red personal recognition security device checked the iris of my eye, my fingerprint, my footprint and the height of my knees. The door clicked open and I entered Z's secret chamber.

Z looked worried, but then he always did. I suppose that when you have the kind of dandruff he had, you're bound to get worried sometimes.

'Sit down, Blond. I've got an important mission for you. One of our agents is missing. We think she's been kidnapped.'

My heart missed a beat. She? Surely it wasn't . . . it couldn't be . . . ?

'I'm afraid it's Goodsole,' Z announced.

'Sophie?' I cried, leaping to my feet, and this time my heart didn't simply miss a beat – it performed three cartwheels and plunged to the pit of my stomach before sliding down my legs and dribbling out between my toes on to the floor.

Z waved a hand at me. 'Blond, I do wish you'd take your bleeding heart somewhere else. Wipe that mess off the floor.'

'I'm sorry, chief. I'm just a bit . . . surprised. How did it happen?'

'Goodsole was trying to infiltrate a gang of Mongolian camel smugglers.'

'Camel smuggling? Why would anyone want to smuggle camels?'

'It's rather disgusting, but very clever. The smugglers get the camels to eat stolen rocket parts. Then they drive the camels over the border, where the camels are killed and the rocket parts retrieved, put back together and sold to other countries.'

'Poor camels.'

'Indeed. Goodsole was about to infiltrate the gang. That was the last we heard from her. She could be keeping a low profile, but we've had news via another agent that Sophie's identity has been revealed and she's been captured, maybe killed. I want you to go to Mongolia, find her and bring her back. Go and see X, collect your equipment and set off immediately. Don't come back without her. This gang is dangerous, Blond. Their leader is Jarvissa the Jugg and he is in league with Deddazzadodo, the head of SNITCH.'

I swallowed. Deddazzadodo, my arch enemy – and he was working with Jarvissa the Jugg, probably the biggest thug in all Asia.

Interview terminated, I hurried down to the lab to find X. He was working on some new gadgets, as usual.

'Now, Blond, listen. This is a watch. Looks like an ordinary watch, doesn't it?'

'Yes.'

'That's because it is an ordinary watch. It tells the time. What do you think?'

'Cunning. I've always wanted a watch that tells the

time. All those other ones you gave me were way too fiddly. They'd explode, squirt gas or fire mini-bullets, take photos, demolish walls, turn into sub-aqua breathing equipment – but I never knew what the right time was.'

'Good. Now this here – this piece of paper – it's absolutely marvellous. With this incredible paper you can fly! As far as Mongolia!'

'You mean it's a plane ticket?'

'Spot on!'

'How fiendishly clever.'

'Quite. Now here is your usual shoulder holster, but the gun is new. My own design, of course. In fact it's not a gun at all, it's a tank.'

'A tank?!'

X gave me a proud smile. 'Well, maybe more of a small tank. A very, very, very small tank. It's remote-controlled, fires six rounds and the shells can pierce marshmallows at a distance of two metres.'

'Deadly,' I said.

'Indeed, and Blond, don't forget to pick up the usual plutonium briefcase which turns into a car, which turns into a nuclear submarine, which turns into a space capsule, which turns into a semi-detached bungalow hideout, will you?'

*

*Twenty-four hours later I was in the
Mongolian desert, looking for camel
smugglers. I had very cleverly
decided to disguise myself as a
camel, a small one which stood
on its back legs all the time. It
wasn't long before a shifty-looking
Mongolian sidled up and offered me a
rocket fin to eat. I pretended to chew on it,
but I didn't swallow and, when he
wasn't looking, I dumped it in a nearby
bin that I almost failed to recognize beneath its woolly
jumper.*

*A large herd of camels had gathered round me,
completing my disguise. It seemed that, even dressed as a
camel, I was still greatly admired. In fact one of the
camels asked me to marry her. By this time the gang had
also appeared and I found myself close enough to hear
their conversation.*

*'Hazz Goodzol brokken her zilenz yet?' (This was
one of the thugs. He was speaking Hill Mongolian
through an array of broken teeth and it came out sounding
rather odd.)*

*'No,' snarled Jarvissa. 'That woman is strong, but
when we start the torture she will soon talk.'*

So! They had captured Sophie and were holding her prisoner. At least she was still alive. But where? And what were they planning to do to her?

'What will they do to her?' I asked.

The entire gang whisked round and stared at me. I coolly hummed an ancient camel hum I just happened to know and looked as uninterested and camel-like as possible.

'I zort one of ze caramels spokk,' muttered the thug, but Jarvissa bellowed with laughter.

'The camel was only humming, you fool! As for the woman, first they will take away her handbag.'

'Urgh! Horrible!'

'Yes. Then they will take the lipstick from the handbag . . .'

'No!'

'. . . and throw it on the fire!'

'Ze spy will nevver zurvive zat. She will zertainly tell uz her zecrets.'

'Yes, indeed she will, but you should get some new teeth. It's almost impossible to understand a word you say. I shall go down to the cave to watch the torture.'

My camel ears pricked up. Aha! So now I knew where Sophie was being held prisoner. I carefully edged away from the other camels and silently trotted down to the cave. There were two guards on the door but because I was a camel they took little notice of me and only asked for the password.

'Let me through,' I muttered (in Mongolian Camelspeak – a language in which I was fluid – there's a lot of spit involved).

The guards parted and I made my way into the cavern. I saw Sophie at once. She was being held in a cage, where she had collapsed on the floor. She looked frail and haggard. I was desperate to comfort her and wanted to throw an arm round her but my arms were nondetachable, and besides, the guards would notice if I suddenly threw one across the room.

Sitting in a chair nearby was none other than the head of SNITCH, Deddazzadodo. My blood ran cold, then hot, then cold. I felt as if I was looking at the Face of Death.

I sidled across to the cage and whispered through the bars.

'It's me, Blond.'

'I know,' she whispered back. 'I recognized you the moment you entered the cave.'

'You recognized me?'

'There's something about the way you walk,' she murmured, and then suddenly she blurted, 'Oh, Blond,

I'm so glad to see you. You've come in the nick of time. Deddazzadodo was about to torture me.'

'I know. He was about to take your handbag away.'

'Oh! The scum!' whimpered Sophie, clutching her little bag even closer.

'Don't worry. I'm here now. I shall save you and your bag. Are you wearing your special exploding Secret Service shoes?' Sophie nodded and I went on. 'I shall create a diversion. As soon as you see them shifting their attention to me, use the explosive to blast open the cage and we shall make our escape.'

'How? They'll come after us.'

'Don't worry. All in good time.'

I left the cage and casually wandered back towards the entrance. As I neared it I reached into my hump and pulled out a collapsible road sign. It bore one word – DIVERSION – and an arrow pointing outside the cave. Without anyone noticing, I stood it on the rocky floor and then left.

Moments later Jarvissa the Jugg entered and saw the sign. 'A diversion!' he shouted to Deddazzadodo, who leapt from his seat with a roar of rage.

'Oh gerbils!' he swore. 'Just when I was going to start the torture!'

'Quick, this way!' cried Jarvissa, following the direction

of the arrow. The gang poured out of the cave and came face to face with yet another road sign, *DIVERSION – THIS WAY*, and more arrows. Off they went, up into the hills, their voices getting fainter and fainter.

All at once there was an almighty explosion from within the cave and smoke billowed from the entrance. I waited for Sophie but she didn't appear. Something must have gone very wrong.

I dashed back inside, almost choking on the smoke and wishing my watch could turn into one of those special breathing apparatus jobbies, but all it would do was tell me that it was ten minutes past five. I found Sophie lying senseless on the floor of the mangled cage. There had been too much explosive in the shoes and when I saw how big her feet were I realized what an easy mistake it was to make. She was size eight – big enough to blow up the Houses of Parliament! She was lucky to be alive.

I lifted Sophie from the floor, draped her over my shoulder then hotfooted it to freedom. Luckily, also in my hump I had an inflatable two-seater, supersonic micro-light, and it wasn't long before we were back home.

Sophie was almost unconscious after her ordeal and I had to carry her into Z's secret chamber.

'Ah, Blond, you're back, and you found Agent Goodsole too. Well done! I don't know what the country would do without you.'

'Probably fall to bits, sir,' I admitted humbly.

Sophie stirred in my arms. 'You saved me,' she whispered.

'I saved your handbag and lipstick too,' I said. 'I told you I would.'

At this point she would have thrown her arms round me but her arms didn't come off either. Instead she lifted her soot-blasted face to mine and kissed me.

'Oh, James!' she breathed.

'Sophie!' I crooned.

'Yuck!' choked Z.

And all that happened on my way home from school. It's true.

9 Strange People in the House

Pete was walking home with me. He was unusually quiet and I asked him if he was all right.

'Yep.'

'Are you coming over this weekend?'

He shrugged.

'What's wrong with you?'

'Nothing.'

'Something's wrong, Pete. You've been like an I-don't-know-what all day.'

He shrugged again. 'I'm fed up, that's all.'

'Come over. Our dads have got plans. They're extending the railway.'

'Oh. Yippee.'

'They're going to knock holes in the wall and build a new bridge across the stairs. The train will go right over our heads.'

'I'm jumping with excitement.'

We had reached my house and stopped at the gate.

For the first time Pete lifted his gaze from the pavement and looked at me guardedly. 'We need to talk,' he said.

'We are talking. We've been talking most of the way home from school.'

'*You've* been talking,' Pete corrected. 'I'll see you later.' He went stomping off down the road, shrouded in mystery. I'd no idea what was up with him, but it was plain that something was on his mind and I was sure it was connected to the new graffiti.

I went up our front path. Dad's car was outside so I knew he'd come home early. He did sometimes because his job had odd hours. I let myself in and raced upstairs to my room. As I passed the door to Mum and Dad's room I heard a thump and automatically glanced in to see what had made it. I got a bit of a shock.

Dad was in there. He had his back to me and he never saw me, but I saw him.

My dad was Wonder Woman.

He had just taken off a long dark wig and was ruffling his hair with his fingers, so I could see it

was him. I was about to speak, but something stopped me. Maybe it was because he'd come home early, or the way he was standing, or the silence in the house, but all at once I knew I wasn't supposed to know. It was a secret.

I crept back downstairs, went to the front door, opened it quietly and then slammed it shut. I called out, 'Hi! I'm back!'

'Tim? I'll be down in a minute. I'm a bit busy.

Put the kettle on, will you, and make a cup of tea?'

I went to the kitchen. What was going on? The real world was being invaded by cartoons. First Harry Franklin's mum appeared in a Peter Rabbit costume. Now my own dad was standing in the bedroom dressed as Wonder Woman.

I heard him come down the stairs, and when he appeared in the kitchen he looked just the same as usual. I was glad about that, but then I found myself wondering *why* I was glad. After all, I'd spent years waiting for Dad to do something exciting, but the moment he appeared in the bedroom as Wonder Woman I got upset.

'Why are you staring at me?' Dad asked.

'Sorry. I had something on my mind.'

'I hear there are problems at school. Graffiti?' I nodded and asked how he knew. 'Mr Dedman sent a letter. I guess it went to all the parents.'

'He's spitting mad,' I chuckled.

'Do you think it's funny?'

'Um, not exactly funny. Maybe more like, fun. Everyone's talking about it. It's exciting. The whole school's perked up. That makes a change.'

'Any idea who's behind it?'

I shook my head. I wasn't going to tell Dad any of my theories about Pete, or Mrs Dove. Dad sipped his tea.

'You know, sometimes it's good when things aren't too exciting,' he told me as he went back upstairs.

'Yes,' I answered, but inside I was thinking: you're only saying that because you are the most unexciting person in the universe. You're only saying that because if anything exciting did ever happen to you, you'd faint on the spot.

Then I found myself going over that image of my father as Wonder Woman. Why had he been dressed like that? I didn't get much chance to think about it because when Mum arrived from the library I got Shock Number Two.

My mum was Snow White.

'Do you like it?' she asked, giving a twirl and then trilling: 'Hi ho!'

'That was the seven dwarfs,' I told her. 'They sang that song.'

'I know, but it was in the same film.'

'Mum, why are you dressed up as Snow White?'

'We're running a children's book promotion at the library – trying to get more young mothers to come in and read with their children. We've been out on the streets the last week or so, handing out leaflets, and we decided to dress up to get more attention.'

Aha! Things were slowly beginning to fall into place. The mystery was clearing. Of course,

Dad had been helping Mum out at the library.

'What are you all dressing up as?' I asked.

'I'm Snow White. Miss Dilly – she runs the children's section – she's The Very Hungry Caterpillar, and Mr Spence, the senior librarian, he's Darth Vader.'

This wasn't what I'd expected at all. 'Don't you have a Peter Rabbit or a Wonder Woman?'

Mum gave me a sharp look. 'No! Why do you ask?'

'I just wondered.'

Mum turned away so I couldn't see her face. 'That would be good, though. Can you get costumes for those? The fancy-dress shop didn't say.'

So, Mum didn't know anything about Dad turning into Wonder Woman. Hmmm. This was very strange, and I was getting worried.

When Pete arrived, I had to tell him, of course. At first he didn't believe me. He reckoned I was making it up just so that I could pretend my dad was interesting.

'I mean, he's not interesting, is he, he's like *my* dad. Listen to them out there, talking trains for hours on end.'

And it was true. My dad and Mr Smith were deeply into the new bridge-building. Dad had knocked through the holes and they had already erected a makeshift bridge and railway track. Tonight they were testing the structure before they set about turning the whole thing into a scale replica of the Forth Bridge.

We watched quietly from my bedroom and listened in as they telephoned each other.

'I'll send the *Duke of Cumberland* through,' my dad said. 'She's the heaviest engine we've got. It'll be a test for the bridge.'

'Good idea. Take it slowly.'

The train whistled and left the station in the bedroom. We heard it trundle across the room. We saw it emerge through the new hole in the wall and out on to the bridge, high above the stairwell – choof choof choof choof.

It reached the centre of the bridge. It lurched, wobbled back, lurched again, and then the whole thing turned into one of those slo-mo images from films: the great engine plunging over the side of the track and into the chasm below, its carriages pouring after it, and then the engine hitting the bridge support and bouncing off, with bits of engine casing and wheels and pistons flying off in every direction, closely followed by the splintering of carriages as they were dragged down by the stricken locomotive, with the bridge itself toppling and crashing from the strain of the whole horrendous accident.

Our dads had rushed to the top of the stairs and they stood and watched, aghast, as the engine came to a halt at the bottom of the stairs, with bits of carriage still landing all around it and the bridge smashing down on top.

Dad picked his way down the stairs, trying not to tread on any debris. At the bottom he lifted up what was left of the engine and examined it closely. He looked up at Mr Smith and shook his head.

Neither of them spoke a word. With one working from the top and the other working his way back up the stairs, they scoured the treads for broken bits, putting all the pieces into a cardboard box. Dad carried it into the spare room. He switched off the light and closed the door. They went downstairs. Mr Smith got his coat and went.

'See you tomorrow?' he said at the door, and Dad nodded silently.

Pete looked at me.

'Blimey,' he said.

'Blimey,' I echoed.

10 The Chickens Strike Again

I never did get to hear what was on Pete's mind.
Our two dads spent the weekend cleaning and
repairing where they could. Even Mum put
away her knitting and helped. It was like they'd
gone into mourning and it made me feel weird.
For the first time I could see how much it all
meant to my dad. It was written right across his
face.

Pete and I had never been able to understand
how our dads could spend so much time simply
sending trains backwards and forwards to each
other without anything happening. And now
something *had* happened – a blistering, obliterat-
ing explosion – and none of us was prepared for
the sheer horror of the cascading trains and
carriages, the noise, the mess . . . the damage.

What was weird was that I just wanted it to go
back to the way it had been before, with the
trains running regularly and safely across the

stairs from one room to another and back.

I tried to take my mind off it all by thinking about my lovely Sophie, although of course she wasn't really mine, or anyone else's for that matter. I wondered if there was someone in class that Sophie did like. I guessed that the most likely person would be Harry. Nick Cartwright could be another. He was good-looking and pretty nifty at football. He was a good swimmer too. He could do backflips into the pool. He made a messy splash, but nobody else even dared try. As for me, well I was on the bottom of everyone's lists for anything.

Everyone knew Sophie wasn't responsible for the graffiti. She'd owned up simply because she was fed up with hanging around in class after school. She knew Mr Dedman would have to let the rest of us go home, and she also knew he'd have to let her go too, because she wasn't even a suspect. Five minutes after we left she followed on.

Monday morning came and everyone was agog to see if the Phantom Scribbler had struck again. Imagine the disappointment when there was nothing to be seen. No fun message, no declarations of love, nothing.

We had IT first thing on Monday. There was one computer room that served the whole school and, since we were first in that morning, we had to switch on and get things going.

Mr Dedman had designed a welcome page for the school computer system. It also acted as a screen saver and basically it was a photo of the school which moved slowly round the screen, along with the words:

𝔚𝔢𝔩𝔠𝔬𝔪𝔢 𝔱𝔬 𝔓𝔢𝔞𝔰𝔢𝔴𝔬𝔬𝔡 𝔍𝔲𝔫𝔦𝔬𝔯 𝔖𝔠𝔥𝔬𝔬𝔩

It was a triumph of Dedhead's imagination.

We filed into the computer room and sat down, two to a computer, and switched on. One by one the screens came up and the giggling began. Mr Dedman's welcome screen had been replaced. Instead there was a picture of several rather manky-looking hens, with the words:

'Interesting,' murmured Mrs Dove. 'Although I don't think Mr Dedman will be all that pleased.'

'Can I show him?' asked Summer, quite ready to shoot off to the head's office and fetch him.

'Not now, Summer,' answered Mrs Dove. 'I shall let him know in due course. Let's just carry on with today's session.'

'What does it mean, anyhow?' grunted Gary Jarvis.

'A good question, Gary,' nodded Mrs Dove. 'Would anyone here like to explain? Vikram?'

'The school is like a battery farm. We're all chickens, crammed in, going over the same things, day in and day out.'

Gary grinned, stuck his fists into his armpits and did his chicken impression again. 'Parrrkk, parrkk, parrkkk.'

'Thank you, Gary,' Mrs Dove said evenly. 'You always make such interesting contributions to class. Well, everyone, the Phantom Scribbler has made a suggestion that you are all chickens. How do you feel about that?'

Things got a bit chaotic for a short while. Some of the class decided that, like Gary, they would actually be chickens, while the rest threw in their comments. It was hardly surprising that most seemed to think that yes, we were.

'We never get a chance to do anything of our own,' Libby pointed out. 'Everything we do is set for us.'

'Yeah, and when we paint a picture it has to be like someone else's. All we ever do are sunflowers and waterlilies and stuff.' This was Harry.

At this point Mr Dedman walked in, complaining about the noise. He wanted to know what was going on.

'We were just discussing the latest contribution from the Phantom Scribbler,' explained Mrs Dove.

'Thank goodness there hasn't been anything new,' growled the head.

Mrs Dove glanced across at the computers. 'Perhaps you should look at this,' she said, clicking back to the welcome page.

Mr Dedman stared. His eyes popped. He rose up on his toes and went down again, clenching his hands. He turned red. 'This is outrageous! Who is responsible for this? I demand to know at once. WHO IS RESPONSIBLE?'

Mrs Dove tried to calm him down. 'I don't think we'll find out this morning. I suppose that in its own way it's quite clever.'

That did it. Mr Dedman really did explode.

'Clever? CLEVER?! Come on then, show me a chicken. SHOW ME A CHICKEN! You can't, can you? Of course not! You haven't even seen one, not even half a chicken. You're just guessing, you useless rabble.'

On and on he went, talking gibberish, you know how some people do. He would stop and we would begin to relax, and all at once he'd set off again, working himself up into yet another rage. Finally he declared the computer room out of bounds to the whole school and sent us back to class.

To make matters worse, there was a message from another teacher, calling Mr Dedman to her class. We discovered later that a message had been left in the TV room. Miss Philpott had pulled the curtains shut, only to find a large piece of paper pinned to the cloth. You couldn't see it until the curtain was pulled across the window. It said:

**Help!
I'm being held prisoner in a chicken shed!**

Poor Mr Dedman! He was beside himself. He didn't know whether to call in the police, MI5, the educational psychiatrist, or what. In the end he held a special meeting with Mrs Dove and some of the school governors. I don't know what went on, but they all looked very serious.

'What do you think they'll do?' I asked Pete, and he shrugged. Ever since the train crash he'd been pretty quiet – in fact, he'd been unusually quiet for some time now – but eventually he said there was bound to be trouble.

'They'll find out in the end.'

'Do you think so?'

Pete nodded and I smiled and shook my head. 'No. Whoever is doing it is too quick. It's almost like they're invisible.'

'Nobody's invisible,' Pete said bluntly.

'The Invisible Man's invisible, otherwise he wouldn't be called The Invisible Man. He'd be The Visible Man, which is stupid, because everyone's visible, so you might just as well call him by his name, Mr Pobble or whatever.'

'Mr Pobble?'

'Or whatever. It could be any name.'

'I'm confused,' Pete complained, wrinkling his nose.

'Me too.'

Just as our conversation seemed to be getting interesting, we were interrupted. The school secretary came over to us in the playground. 'Morning, boys. Tim, could you pop into Mr Dedman's office before you go back to class? He'd like a quick word.'

'Sure.' I gave her a tight smile. 'What's it about?'

'No idea,' she said. The bell went for the end of break. I raised my eyebrows and looked at Pete. His face had drained of colour.

'I'd better go,' I said.

'Yep.' There was a pause and then he said, 'It wasn't me.' What was he on about? I knew it wasn't him.

Mr Dedman was not alone in his office. Mrs Dove was there and a couple of other people. One was a school governor. The other was Mrs Bolton from the newsagent's. Everyone looked very serious – all except Mr Dedman, who had a kind of grim smile on his face.

'We want to show you something, Tim. Let's go along to the TV room, shall we?'

The curtains were still pulled and the notice pinned up. The head tore it down crossly and stuffed it in the waste-paper bin. I remember thinking: Heavens! A bin that Mum hasn't plastered with shells. Must be the last one in the galaxy!

'Take a look at this, Tim. It's a video. It belongs to Mrs Bolton here. She runs the shop just outside the school.'

'Yes, I know.'

'You may remember the shop was robbed a few months ago.'

'Yes.'

'And after the robbery a CCTV camera was put up nearby, just to keep an eye on things.' Mr Dedman's eyes were boring into my skull like high-speed drill bits. Tungsten carbide tips.

'Oh.'

'And this morning Mrs Bolton happened to take a look at the tape.'

Mr Dedman bent forward and inserted the tape into the video machine. He pressed the remote. The film was in black and white. It was very dark because it was night-time. Even so, you could clearly make out the small figure of a child heading along the school wall, opposite Mrs Bolton's shop. The child reached the lowest point of the wall and clambered up. It was impossible to see who it was, but as the mystery figure swivelled to drop down into the school playground, the face was illuminated by a nearby street lamp and all was revealed.

11 Hurrah for Marka?

I am Marka, The Nightwriter. Like a shadow, like the passage of a dark cloud in a moonless sky, unseen, I make my way through the glistening wet streets. I see the hunting cats, hear the owl and note the passing of the fox, for we are all Creatures Of The Dark. But only I am The Nightwriter, the one that can write!

I break open the prisons of our minds and there I leave my sign, like Zorro, except that I can do the complete alphabet and not just the letter Z. I set the mind free! For I am Marka, The Nightwriter, and none may know my true name.

What drives me on? What makes me face such danger? What makes me the swashbuckling hero of liberty? What is a swash, and how do you buckle it?

I will tell you what drives me on. It is an image of beauty, my own love, The Last Wild Spirit – Sophie. Somehow I have to tell her what I feel, for one day surely our two hearts will beat as one.

There is danger all around, not least from the evil

*Lord Mankyhand Dedloss in his castle of boiling rock,
for he has imprisoned The Last Wild Spirit in The
Black Pit, his deepest dungeon, where no light penetrates
the gloom and no mortal man may enter.*

*But I shall overcome such perils and dangers for I am
Marka, The Nightwriter, and I go where no one dares
go, and often get into terrible trouble because of it.*

*See! Here comes Lord Mankyhand Dedloss now, with
his one eye, his giant pit bull hound, Garyjugg, and his
Sword of Destiny, the mightiest sword in the land, stolen
from the Elves of Plinky-plop-land. (He wanted a ring
but stole the sword instead.)*

*First I climb the outer castle wall, like a silent spider.
Lightly my feet dance across the stony ground to the very
wall of Lord Mankyhand Dedloss's home. I take my
green magic marker and there I place my magic mark, for
truth will be revealed.*

There! I have done the deed! Hastily I make my exit. I scale the wall and slip through an unfastened window. I slip past endless gloom-filled rooms, each one crammed with hundreds of hunched creatures, toiling over their work like battery chickens, scratching at paper with their pens, answering endless questionnaires. These are The Deddend, the thousands of ex-mortals that Lord Dedloss has turned into his zombie servants, who have no will of their own and must obey his every command.

And now Dedloss has captured the one surviving mortal, The Last Wild Spirit, and once he has taken her good soul, the light will go from the land altogether. As silent as a panther I descend the stairs, penetrating the very bowels of the ancient castle.

I hear sobbing, and there, huddled in a damp corner, is Sophie, The Last Wild Spirit. My heart goes out to her, she looks so wretched. I call to her softly and she turns. Despite her tears she smiles, a smile of such radiance it is like a million angels singing to me.

'Oh Nightwriter!' she cries with joy. 'I knew you would come and rescue me!'

'It had to be done,' I answer quietly. 'But you really should stop getting into all these scrapes.'

'Hurry, we must make good our escape.'

'Yes, but first I have something to do.'

*So saying, I take up my pen once more and write on
the wall of the prison:*

*But hark! Garyjugg is barking. Have we been discovered?
Has the wretched hound caught my scent? I hear footsteps.
I cling to the shadows, pushing Sophie back against the
damp darkness of the wall and praying that the danger
will pass – but it does not.*

*Lord Mankyhand Dedloss is carrying a flaming brand
which lights the whole room. In an instant he has spotted
us and drawn his weapon, the great two-handled Sword
of Destiny, Blade of Death, Slayer of Life, Snuffer of
Light and many other similarly silly titles.*

*'Why, 'tis The Nightwriter himself, come to save The
Last Wild Spirit! How sweet! Trying to escape, eh?
Well, well, well! I have you trapped and now you shall*

both die, for I am going to skewer you with my mighty Sword of Death.'

'Blade of Death,' I corrected. 'Sword of Destiny and Blade of Death. You're getting muddled, Dedloss.'

'I care not a jot, footling fool, for my two greatest enemies are about to be slivered like slices of salami!'

'Oh, painful,' mewed Sophie, blanching.

'Do not blanch, Sophie, for I shall fight the Blade of Death with the Magic Marker of Truth!'

'Pah! Magic Marker of Truth? What use will that be against my keen blade? Prepare to die, Nightwriter, for I shall make pâté of your liver.' And so saying, Dedloss hurled himself at me, taking great wind-whistling slices with his sword. But every time he lunged at me I took my marker and I scribbled as fast as I could, again and again:

MISSED!
MISSED!

'Damn you, Nightwriter!' bellowed Dedloss. 'You are too quick for me. Even so, I don't think you will be able to do anything about this.'

All at once he cast his sword aside, drew a pistol and, pointing it straight at my heart, he pulled the trigger. But before it could go 'Bang!' I wrote 'Phutt!' and instead of whizzing out of the barrel at top speed, the bullet simply dribbled to the end, trickled out and fell on the floor with a tiny 'Ting'. (Which I didn't even bother to write.)

'Raaargh and double raaargh!' roared Dedloss. 'You may think you have got the better of me, Nightwriter, but you seem to have forgotten my faithful pit bull, Garyjugg. While you have been busy fighting me, Garyjugg has carried off your true love!'

I groaned. Not again. That Sophie was a real liability – always in a scrape. It was a jolly good thing I loved her. I raced after the disappearing hound. Garyjugg was bounding ahead with Sophie in his jaws, flopping about like a rag doll and screaming with terror. Putting on a burst of speed, I flung myself on to the hound's hairy back and soon we were rolling across the ground, over and over, in a mighty tussle. I grabbed the beast's jaws, forcing them open.

Sophie, now released from the jaws of the slavering beast, stood to one side and watched. From time to time she went 'Oooh!' or 'Ah!' as Garyjugg sank his fearsome teeth into my arm, leg, head, bottom, whatever. But I felt no pain, despite being gnashed to ribbons and covered in my own blood, for my whole being was concentrated upon saving the The Last Wild Spirit.

Who knows how long the battle would have continued had I not suddenly recalled an old trick taught me by Wickenthing, the Elfin Sage, when I had sat at his feet as a child. As Garyjugg bellowed with rage, I seized my opportunity, plunging my fist and arm right into the monster hound's mouth, down his throat, down to his very intestines, and there I grabbed his innards and twisted and scrunged until his eyes watered like Niagara, and with a terrible yelp he ran for his life.

I was free! I seized Sophie's hand and began to drag her up the winding steps, but now there came to our ears a spine-chilling rustling as ten thousand zombie Deddends came after us, creeping, crawling, walking, running, leaping, jumping, dancing – they came after us in every way imaginable, spurred on by the commands of Lord Mankyhand Dedloss.

'After them, my slaves! Tear them to pieces, for love and freedom will not triumph while there is breath in my body!'

'Hurry!' I called to Sophie. 'Don't give up now.'

And then all at once it was over.

A great, crooked shadow fell upon us and it was as if every atom of power had been sucked from our muscles, turning them to jelly, and we could move no further, for towering over us were The Almighty Three, the Supreme Elders from The Land of Geriatrica, who had the wisdom of the centuries locked in their gnarled and walnut-like skulls.

Now they stood in judgement over us and we were all helpless beneath their stern gaze. The eldest of the Elders, Boltonbaggis, blind but for her all-seeing eye that could even pierce the deepest gloom of night, stepped forward.

'Marka, The Nightwriter, you have been found wanting.' Her voice was like the voice of a thousand hidden accusers and it set my body quaking with fear.

12 The End of the World Gets Closer

It was me. It would have been stupid to deny it. I sat in silence, my eyes fixed on the frozen image of myself on the TV screen. Mr Dedman was seething.

'I thought it was you, right from the beginning,' he hissed. 'You said it wasn't.'

'I was lying,' I muttered.

The head teacher straightened up and looked at the others. 'I knew it was him all along.'

'Really?' This came from Mrs Dove. 'What are we going to do then?' she asked. I thought she looked even older than usual.

Mr Dedman rubbed his hands together. 'I don't think there's much question about that. Tim has been nothing but a problem for years. He should be expelled, instantly.'

It was like the ground disappearing beneath my feet. Expelled!

OK, I am sure you are thinking: You're such

an idiot, Tim. What do you expect to happen if you go around doing something like that? It's madness. You know it's creating big trouble and in the end it will just make even bigger trouble for yourself.

Of course I knew all that. But I never expected to be expelled. Chucked out. Thoughts were rushing through my brain, piling up in a chaotic log-jam of disaster. I'm ashamed to say my knees were trembling and my legs felt like porridge. Someone put a hand on my shoulder.

'You'd better sit down, Tim,' said Mrs Dove. 'This might take a while to sort out.'

'He can stand,' snapped Mr Dedman. 'He's a troublemaker. Don't sympathize with him.'

'If Tim doesn't sit down, he'll fall down,' Mrs Dove answered evenly, pushing me into a chair.

Mr Dedman rolled his eyes in disbelief. The school governor, Mr Moore, asked the head what he thought they should do next.

'Expel him!' repeated Mr Dedman incredulously. 'It's obvious. The boy's a complete waste of space. He's a vandal, a vandal with a capital V. He should not be in school. He's a bad example. He's wasting everyone's time.'

'Mr Dedman!' Mrs Dove cut in sharply. 'We should not be discussing this here and now.'

'Oh, really? I am so sorry. I was under the mistaken impression that I was the head teacher here and that I made the decisions, Mrs Dove, not you.'

'Nevertheless this is not the time or place. The matter needs to go before all the governors. Such an important decision cannot be made here and now.'

'Mrs Dove is right,' muttered Mr Moore. 'We do need to call a meeting of all the governors to decide this issue.'

'Right. Right. Right then.' Words spat like bullets from the head's mouth.

All this was going on above my head. I listened in, amazed. It was like walking in on an intergalactic starship battle, with phasers going off in every direction and bodies falling to the ground all around you.

Mr Dedman was breathing heavily. I felt that what he really wanted to do was kill me there and then and he was really, really fed up that he couldn't.

'In that case I want him sent home at once. I

want him excluded until the governors meet to
decide his fate and I am telling you now that he
has got to go!'

'I'll ask the secretary to ring home,' offered
Mr Moore. 'Maybe his mother or father can
collect him.'

'Will one of them be at home?' Mrs Dove
asked me quietly.

'Mum will be at the library, but she'll be able
to come and collect me.' I said this, but it was
the last thing I wanted, to have my parents
involved. I was slowly beginning to realize that

everything was out in the open now. The whole world would soon know.

'For goodness' sake get him out of my sight,' urged Mr Dedman.

'I'll take him to the medical room. We'll wait for his parents there.' Mrs Dove took my arm and led me away. As we crossed the hall and headed down the long corridor that led to the medical room, I was aware of faces pressed against classroom doors, looking at me, staring.

Both my hands were manacled to a heavy chain that passed twice around my wrists. I could barely raise my arms, because of the sheer weight of the chain. A further shackle rattled between my legs, connecting with the heavy links that manacled my ankles together. I could not walk, but could only take short, staggering steps, sometimes tripping on the shackle.

The passageway was lined with jeering faces. People waved and called out, their faces ugly with mocking laughter. I was the victim of a living nightmare.

Ahead of me now I could see the scaffold, towering above. Lightning raged, thunder cracked, the rain poured relentlessly upon my head, a billion tears shed by a weeping sky.

The notorious executioner, Deadheader, stood on the platform while his assistant, Juggerjab, tied a blindfold around the executioner's eyes. The full horror of my fate struck home. I was to be beheaded by a blindfolded executioner! Deadheader's massive hands calmly rested on the long thick handle of the axe that had taken the lives of so many. And now it was to be my turn . . .

Mrs Dove pushed open the door. I went in and collapsed on the bed. She shut the door quietly and then sat down at my side.

'I blame myself,' she said suddenly. 'I should have stopped you.'

I frowned. 'You couldn't. You didn't know.'

'No, not for sure, but I did have an idea it was you.'

'Why? How?'

Mrs Dove smiled and shrugged. 'I don't know, Tim. I suppose it might have something to do with the stories you write in class – that is, when we have time to write whole stories. There was something in the graffiti messages that seemed similar.'

'So why *didn't* you say anything?'

Mrs Dove stood up. She went to the door. She paced the room a couple of times and the silence in the room grew heavier and heavier until I thought we would both be squashed dead beneath its weight. Finally she stopped pacing, turned and faced me.

'Because, to put it simply, I agree with you. We *are* like battery chickens in this school, even the teachers, and it makes me so angry.' She gave me a flicker of a smile. 'The thing is, Tim, although I agree with what you think, I don't agree with what you did. I understand why you did it, but it was wrong.'

'I know that, but I . . . I couldn't stop.' I gave a faint laugh. 'I was Marka, The Nightwriter.'

Mrs Dove looked at me quizzically. 'Marka, the Nightwriter?'

'Yes. He's like Zorro. He goes about doing good but, instead of fighting evil with his sword, he has a magic marker and he leaves messages.'

'You were Marka, with his magic marker?'

We looked at each other, eye to eye. Mrs Dove's face began to crinkle at the edges. I could feel bubbles of air squeezing up behind my nose. Her mouth started to twitch. I pressed my lips together as hard as I could.

But nothing worked for either of us. We both burst out laughing at the same moment, and to me it felt like for months I had been drowning, drowning, drowning, sinking deeper and deeper into the depths of a cold, sunless ocean, and now suddenly I had shot straight back to the surface, bursting out into the warm air and

sunshine, drawing great gulps of life-giving air.

We laughed and laughed until we heard footsteps coming down the corridor. Mrs Dove's finger flew to her lips. 'Sssh!'

When the secretary came in, we looked reasonably serious, I suppose, though she did give us one or two odd glances. Behind her was Snow White. Mum looked pale and edgy, but at least she didn't plough straight into telling me off.

'You'd best come home,' she said rather stiffly.

'Sorry about all this, Mum.'

'Yes, well, we'll talk about it when your father gets in.'

Mrs Dove said she would ring my parents in the evening and talk things through with them. 'There's a lot you need to know,' she advised Mum before turning to me. 'I'll help you all I can, Tim. Don't be too downhearted.'

I could only nod. As we went, Snow White rummaged in her bag and suddenly produced a small bowl, covered with tiny shells. She thrust it at the secretary.

'I thought you could keep paper clips in it,' she said.

The secretary looked somewhat surprised but smiled and took the little gift. I was gobsmacked. Here I was, being excluded from school, and Mum was handing over shell-encrusted pots for paper clips.

'Well, goodbye then,' she said, pushing me towards the door, and off we went. It felt like I was leaving school for the last time. I kept thinking, this is the last time I shall ever walk down here. This is the last time I shall ever cross this hall. This is the last time I shall ever go past the head's office (thank goodness). This is the last time I shall go down these stairs, and I shall never see Sophie Goodsole again.

I shall never see Sophie Goodsole again!

13 Dad's Story

There was no doubt about it. Mum and Dad
were cross. However, they were not as cross as I
had expected. Not only that, but just when they
were right in the middle of doing their cross bit
(you know, where they say things like: 'What
were you thinking of? How could you let us
down like this? Don't you know how much
damage you've caused? What on earth gave you
the idea? Have you been drinking too much
cola, orange food-colouring, sniffing felt tips?
Did someone put you up to it?' etc., etc., etc. –
you know what I mean) – the phone rang.

It was Mrs Dove. I was sent out of the room
so I couldn't hear anything, but Mrs Dove was
on the phone for ages. Eventually Mum called
me back in.

'It seems you have a champion,' she said.

'I don't understand.'

'Mrs Dove says that there are reasons why you

did what you did and no doubt things will become clearer at the meeting with the governors and the head teacher. Your father agrees. I'm not sure that I do, Tim, but I trust your father's judgement and I trust Mrs Dove. She's a fine teacher and I hope you haven't disappointed her.'

Yes. I hoped so too.

Waiting for that meeting with the governors was bad, really bad. I was at home and I had nothing to do except watch Mum sticking shells on our wheelie bin. (She'd given up knitting when she realized she'd forgotten to knit a neck opening for her swing-bin jumper, so she couldn't actually put anything in the bin.)

'I've never attempted anything as big as this,' she told me excitedly. I was beginning to think that if I stood still long enough she'd start sticking shells all over me too. And Dad. We'd be like monsters out of some horror movie:

They came from the bottom of the sea – INVASION OF THE SHELL-SHOCKERS! See them turn humans into walking, shell-covered zombies! See them snap off arms and legs and heads with their giant lobster claws! Shell-shockers! Is there one in your home right now?

I spent ages going over what might happen to me. What would happen if I was expelled? Would I be sent to another school where I didn't know anyone? Would any other school want me when they heard what I had done?

I desperately wanted to talk it through with someone, but I couldn't talk with Mum or Dad, and Pete wasn't allowed in the house after what I'd done.

'Maybe after the meeting you boys can get back together,' said Dad. 'I know it's hard,' he added. 'Things will work out. Sometimes things aren't as bad as they seem.'

Oh yeah, Dad, right.

Strangely enough, Dad seemed to know what I was thinking. 'Hmmm. Maybe that sounds a bit daft.'

'A bit?'

'A lot?'

'A lot,' I nodded, giving him a wan smile.

'I was speaking from experience,' he said. 'When I was twelve I did something a lot worse.'

'Really?' I wondered what was coming next. My dad, the most boring dad in the world, did something truly terrible when he was twelve. I wondered what it could be. Spilled his orange juice? Jumped on the best sofa? Shouted 'Knickers!' at the vicar?

'I was at my friend Jason's house. His parents were out. I can't remember why they weren't there. Anyhow, Jason said why not drive his mum's car up the track? They lived next to a farm and there was a track running alongside the house, right up into the fields. So we went to the garage and Jason said, "I know how to drive. Do you?" I didn't want to be shown up, so I said, "Course I know how to drive! I'm not an idiot!" And Jason says, "Can you do reverse?" And I say, "Course I can!"'

'Could you?'

'Of course not. I was only twelve. Tall for my age, but still only twelve.'

'What happened?'

'I got in Jason's mum's car and started it up. That was easy. I put it into reverse. That was easy too. I took off the handbrake and let out the clutch. The car shot backwards, straight into the corner of the garage.'

'It never!'

'Yes. Bang! Straight into the corner of the garage.'

'Blimey.'

'Yes, blimey,' echoed Dad, turning a little red.

'What happened when they found out?'

'Hang on, I haven't finished yet. When the car shot backwards it demolished the pillar holding up the corner, and the garage roof came crashing down on top of the car. And there I was, stuck. The car wouldn't budge. The doors wouldn't open. I couldn't get out. Jason simply vanished

and I had to sit there until his parents came
home. They weren't very pleased.'

'You were in trouble?'

'Deep, deep trouble,' Dad said quietly, slipping
an arm round my shoulders. 'It'll be all right,
Tim. You did something wrong, but you're not
the first and you won't be the last, and besides,
there are other people
who have some
explaining to do as
well.'

'How do you mean?'

'You'll find out soon
enough.'

There was
something I wanted
to ask him. I had
been holding back
for ages but I
couldn't keep it to
myself any longer.
'Dad, I know the
secret identity of
Wonder Woman.'

I felt the arm

round my shoulder stiffen with surprise. Then it
relaxed again.

'Have you told anyone?'

'Only Pete.'

'Has he said anything to anyone?'

'No.'

'Good. Don't tell a soul, Tim. Not a soul.'

'Why not?' I was bursting with curiosity. Dad
made it sound so mysterious.

'You'll find out soon, I promise.'

So it was hard, waiting, and Dad's story had
given me quite a lot to think about. It was pretty
difficult imagining my dad as a twelve-year-old,
doing something like that. But I guess we're all
hiding secrets of one sort or another.

Dad was supposed to come to the governors'
meeting with Mum and me, but in the end he
couldn't make it. I was very disappointed. After
the story about the car I knew he understood
how I felt. Anyhow, he explained that he couldn't
make the beginning, but that he'd try and get
there as soon as possible.

The meeting had been fixed for ten o'clock in
the morning. Dad had gone to work at about
eight, and that left Mum and myself sitting

around, nervously twiddling our thumbs. Then at nine o'clock there was a terrible banging on the front door, like an elephant in desperate need of a lavatory. It wasn't an elephant. It was Pete.

'You'd better come to school,' he puffed, breathless from running. 'You have just got to see what's going on.'

'He can't,' my mum answered. 'He's excluded. You know that, Peter.'

'It's very important. Honest, Mrs Witkinson. Mrs Dove said it'd be all right. She said to come quickly.'

Mum grabbed her coat and we set off, half walking, half running. Pete was still panting but he managed a few words.

'It wasn't me that told on you,' he gasped. And I suddenly remembered he'd said something like that before. 'It wasn't me.'

'Nobody told on me, Pete. I was caught on CCTV. Anyhow, you didn't know.'

'But I did. I saw you, late one evening. It wasn't all that long after we followed Harry; do you remember? Only this time I followed you. You were behaving oddly, so I kept an eye out. I saw you get over the wall and that was when I knew it was you. But I didn't tell.'

'Thanks. I mean it. Thanks, Pete.'

By this time we'd reached the school. At the gates the first thing we saw was that the playground was full. Everyone was there: the teachers, all the children, the assistants, the secretary, the caretaker.

And then we saw the walls. Everywhere was covered with graffiti. Messages had been left on every surface.

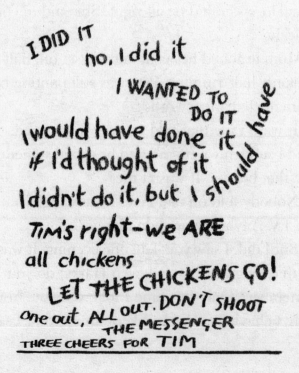

I DID IT
no, I did it
I WANTED TO
DO IT
I would have done it
if I'd thought of it
I didn't do it, but I should have
TIM'S right – we ARE
all chickens
LET THE CHICKENS GO!
one out, ALL OUT. DON'T SHOOT
THE MESSENGER
THREE CHEERS FOR TIM

Not only were the messages there, but they were all signed, and standing around beneath them was my entire class. They had lined up under the wall and they simply stood there. Every single one was holding either a paintbrush or a can of spray-paint. They were all grinning. Even Juggernaut Jarvis.

I didn't know where to look. One by one I read the messages until my heart suddenly stopped. It rose up in my throat and almost jumped out. I had just read:

SOPHIE
4
TIM
SG

And it was signed.
By her.

14 Surprise! Surprise!

A moment later I saw Mr Dedman. Come to think of it, I heard him before I saw him. He was shouting. (Not like him!) He was bellowing. He was striding up and down, waving his arms, almost beside himself. When he spotted me, his face underwent so many changes I thought his eyeballs would fall right out and his ears explode. But he couldn't say a word. Just for once I hadn't done anything.

Instead, he began yelling at Mrs Dove as if she was personally responsible for the fact that her class had just given the school wall a major makeover. He roared at the kids. Gary and some of his gang were making quiet chicken noises. I don't know what he would have done if two of the governors hadn't turned up and gently led him away. As he went into the school he looked back over his shoulder at me.

'I'll see you inside, Witkinson. Don't think

you're going to get away with this!'

Get away with what, I wondered.

My mother wasn't sure what to make of it all. 'I don't know what's going on,' she said, at least three times. Mrs Dove came over as soon as Mr Dedman was out of sight. I could tell she was excited, but trying to keep control of herself.

'It was like this when I arrived,' she beamed. 'There's more round the other side of the school. Poor Mr Dedman doesn't know what to do. There are so many people involved he doesn't know where to start.' She sighed and turned to me. 'We're keeping our fingers crossed for you, Tim. As you can see, you have quite a lot of supporters. Well, it looks like the rest of the governors are arriving. You'd better go inside.'

'I don't understand why the whole class thinks it's OK to write on the school wall,' murmured Mum. 'It's not on the new curriculum, is it?'

Mrs Dove laughed and shook her head. 'I don't think so, Mrs Witkinson, but if it is, then my class certainly doesn't need any practice.'

We had almost reached the door when I felt a hand on my arm. It was Sophie. Her eyes were shining. 'Thank you,' she whispered.

'What are you thanking *me* for?'

'You saved me from Juggernaut. I'll be waiting for you outside. Good luck.'

I took a deep breath and stepped inside. The door closed behind us, and suddenly all was quiet and the air seemed to fill with gloom and doom. It was as if the walls themselves were leaning towards us, wagging their fingers (if they had fingers) and saying, 'Make sure you behave.'

The meeting was held in the Staff Room. Chairs had been placed in a big circle. At the top end of the circle was a large desk and behind that sat Mr Dedman and the chair of governors.

Mr Dedman started everything off by apologizing for the 'dreadful' scenes outside, claiming that I had put the whole class up to it. I tried to explain that as far as I was concerned I didn't even have any friends in the class, apart from Pete, but Mr Dedman wasn't listening. He'd got the idea fixed in his head that it was my fault. I might have been a million miles away at the time; I might have been dead a thousand years; whatever, it was still my fault. At this point my mum got cross and stood up.

'Excuse me, Mr Dedman, but Tim had no hand in that display outside. He has been at home the last few days because you excluded him from school.'

'Have you ever heard of the telephone, Mrs Witkinson?' he sneered back.

'I have been at home with him. He hasn't used the telephone.'

'Oh? And what about his mobile?'

'He doesn't have a mobile.'

'Walkie-talkie.'

'He doesn't have one of those either.'

'WELL, MAYBE HE SENT CARRIER

PIGEONS!' roared the head, and everyone sat way back in their chairs and stared at him, until at length he mumbled, 'Sorry, bit carried away for a moment.' He sat down and drummed his fingers on the table.

Mum opened her bag and began to rummage around. I started a prayer: *Dear God, please don't let Mum get out a shell-covered pot for Mr Dedman's biros, please.* But she only wanted a tissue to blow her nose.

The meeting went on and on. An hour had already passed and Dad still hadn't appeared. I wished he was there. At least he understood. Mr Dedman trotted out a list of my crimes. He produced photographs of the messages I had left. They were passed from one governor to

another. I watched their faces. They looked horrified. I heard mutterings amongst them and I knew I was going to be executed.

Mr Dedman began to wind up his speech. He pointed out that I had been in the school almost four years and had contributed nothing. I didn't play for a single team. I was useless at sport. Look at all the cups the school had won. Had I helped? No way. Had I demonstrated even the ability to produce good work? No. He seized a scruffy sheet of paper from the table in front of him.

'Here is a typical example of the boy's work,' Mr Dedman complained. 'This is a recent piece. Along with the rest of the class he was asked to write a poem on a subject I myself had carefully chosen, and this is what he wrote:

A Two-minute Poem about *Wednesday*
by Tim Witkinson

Wednesday is a stupid title for a poem.
Poems should not be about
Days of the Week.
Poems should be about heroes
and triumphs and disasters,
bravery and butchery, love and death,
laughing and crying and living.
Wednesday is a stupid title for a poem.
But not as stupid as Tuesday.
Anyhow, you can't write a good poem in two
minutes.

'It's nonsense!' shouted Mr Dedman.' It doesn't even rhyme! That child is bad through and through, and he's corrupting the children around him.'

The head teacher came out from behind the desk and stood right in front of me, his eyes stabbing into me, twisting like thin knives in my guts. A tight, cruel smile played across his lips. 'In fact,' said Mr Dedman, 'you only have to look out of this window at that dreadful wall of graffiti below to see exactly what kind of evil influence Tim has had on his classmates. We cannot tolerate this level of insubordination and vandalism in this school. HE MUST GO!'

All around the room I could see governors half nodding, leaning towards each other and exchanging whispered words. Several of them threw quick glances at me, and in their eyes I could see my own shame, and my fate.

And Dad wasn't there. Just when I really needed him.

Then the staff-room door suddenly banged open and in burst – Peter Rabbit?

Was it Peter Rabbit? Yes it was, except that he didn't exactly burst in because his costume got jammed in the door frame and someone behind had to push and push before Peter hurtled forward into the room, tripped over his own feet, went head over heels across three governors in their armchairs, and fell to the floor in the middle of the circle.

Close behind came Wonder Woman. She (He? It?) stood there, blocking the door, looking straight at Mr Dedman.

'David Donald Derek Dedman, I arrest you for the unlawful storage and selling of frozen chickens which have been condemned by food standards officers. You are also charged with using school premises for unlawful activities. Have you anything to say?'

Mr Dedman couldn't speak. His jaw moved. His lips smacked about a bit, but basically he was speechless. So was I. My head teacher had just been arrested by Wonder Woman and Peter Rabbit.

My dad! The hero! He'd saved me! Result!

And that was more or less it.

Mr Dedman was taken away, with Wonder Woman gripping one arm and Peter Rabbit the other. At the door he turned and threw me a bewildered look.

'You never saw a single chicken, did you? You didn't know at all.'

I shook my head. His head sank in defeat and that was the last I saw of him.

Dad came back a few minutes later, once he'd handed Mr Dedman over to the police, and explained everything to the stunned panel of governors. It seemed that Dad's job was exactly what he'd always told me, but with several bits added which he'd kept very quiet about. He worked for the Food Standards Agency, which of course makes it all sound very boring. That was deliberate, according to Dad, because nobody was supposed to know what he did. He was an undercover officer and he often worked on quite hairy things, where people could get nasty and so on, so it was kept pretty hush-hush.

The problem was that this particular case was very close to home. That was one reason why he and his partner – yes, you guessed, Mrs

Franklin, alias Peter Rabbit – had dressed up. They reckoned it would be a really good way of keeping watch on the chicken gang without them suspecting anything.

'And it worked a treat,' laughed Dad. 'I got the idea when your mother told me about the special book promotion the library was planning. I thought it would look like we were part of that and the criminals wouldn't suspect a thing.'

It turned out that Mr Dedman was one of the leaders of a small gang that were taking frozen chickens that had been declared unfit for human consumption and selling them back to supermarkets. They were actually using the freezers in the school kitchens to store thousands of chickens over the last few months.

So that explained how Dedman was able to drive a posh Porsche and, of course, why he got his knickers in such a terrible twist when I started to leave graffiti about chickens all over the school!

As for me, the governors decided to give me another chance. Many of them had been receiving complaints for some time from both parents and staff about Mr Dedman's supercontrol of the school. It was time the school was placed in more caring hands, so the governors made Mrs Dove the new head teacher.

Everything changed. School was soon full of laughter and excitement. We wrote WHOLE stories! We painted battles and dinosaurs! The battery-farm chickens had gone free-range at last. And I sat next to Sophie Goodsole.

I even began to understand something about Dad and the trains. You see, I reckon Dad plays with those trains because, after a hard day playing hide-and-seek with criminals, all he wants to do is relax with something very straightforward, safe and predictable.

I go upstairs with him sometimes. Not every night, of course. I'm not *that* weird. But we've rebuilt the Forth Bridge – Dad, me, Pete and his dad. Mum says it's OK but the bridge would look a lot nicer if she stuck some shells on it.

Tim Witkinson groaned. Would there be no end to his despair? He stood on the executioner's platform, with a bitter cold wind blowing upon him, whilst Deadheader sharpened his great axe.

'There will be no escape for you this time,' laughed the executioner. 'You have been well and truly caught and now you shall perish. Lay your head upon the chopping block.'

I felt sick to the pit of my stomach. Juggerjab, the executioner's assistant, forced me to my knees and laid my head upon the block. In silence I said my goodbyes: 'Goodbye, Mum; goodbye, Dad; goodbye, trains; goodbye, shelly things; goodbye, sky; goodbye, trees; goodbye, world; goodbye, Sophie. Oh, Sophie, my True Love!'

I heard Deadheader raise the axe. I closed my eyes tight. Every muscle in my body stiffened with fear.

All at once there was an outcry from the crowd. 'Look! Look!' I heard a tremendous commotion and opened one eye. There were Wonder Woman and Peter Rabbit, speeding down towards us, and close behind was The Dove.

Wonder Woman seized Deadheader by the shoulders and carried him away, up into the sky. 'Your reign of terror is over, Deadheader!' cried Wonder Woman. 'And everyone shall be free!'

'Hurrah! Hurrah!' yelled the crowd.

Peter Rabbit simply threw herself upon Juggerjab and squashed him flat. Meanwhile The Dove gently raised me from the chopping block and placed a warm coat around my shoulders. Together we left the terrible platform and went into the crowd. A passage amongst the people opened up before us and then I saw, standing at the far end, waiting with arms outstretched, Sophie Goodsole. My Sophie.

The Dove gave me a gentle push forward. I walked towards her. I walked faster. I started to run. And then we were together.

'Sophie,' I murmured.

'Tim,' she breathed.

'Oh, Sophie!'

'Oh, Tim!'

And then I woke up.

Ask Jeremy

Of all the books you have written, which one is your favourite?

I loved writing both **KRAZY KOW SAVES THE WORLD – WELL, ALMOST** and **STUFF**, my first book for teenagers. Both these made me laugh out loud while I was writing and I was pleased with the overall result in each case. I also love writing the stories about Nicholas and his daft family – **MY DAD**, **MY MUM**, **MY BROTHER** and so on.

If you couldn't be a writer what would you be?

Well, I'd be pretty fed up for a start, because writing was the one thing I knew I wanted to do from the age of nine onward. But if I DID have to do something else, I would love to be either an accomplished pianist or an artist of some sort. Music and art have played a big part in my whole life and I would love to be involved in them in some way.

What's the best thing about writing stories?

Oh dear – so many things to say here! Getting paid for making things up is pretty high on the list! It's also something you do on your own, inside your own head – nobody can interfere with that. The only boss you have is yourself. And you are creating something that nobody else has made before you. I also love making my readers laugh and want to read more and more.

Did you ever have a nightmare teacher?
(And who was your best ever?)

My nightmare at primary school was Mrs Chappell, long since dead. I knew her secret – she was not actually human. She was a Tyrannosaurus rex in disguise. She taught me for two years when I was in Y5 and Y6, and we didn't like each other at all. My best ever was when I was in Y3 and Y4. Her name was Miss Cox, and she was the one who first encouraged me to write stories. She was brilliant. Sadly, she is long dead too.

When you were a kid you used to play kiss-chase. Did you always do the chasing or did anyone ever chase you?!

I usually did the chasing, but when I got chased, I didn't bother to run very fast! Maybe I shouldn't admit to that! We didn't play kiss-chase at school – it was usually played during holidays. If we had tried playing it at school we would have been in serious trouble. Mind you, I seemed to spend most of my time in trouble of one sort or another, so maybe it wouldn't have mattered that much.

14½ Things You Didn't Know About

Jeremy Strong

* * * * * * * * * * * * * * * *

1. He loves eating liquorice.

2. He used to like diving. He once dived from the high board and his trunks came off!

3. He used to play electric violin in a rock band called **THE INEDIBLE CHEESE SANDWICH**.

4. He got a 100-metre swimming certificate when he couldn't even swim.

5. When he was five, he sat on a heater and burnt his bottom.

6. Jeremy used to look after a dog that kept eating his underpants. (No – **NOT** while he was wearing them!)

7. When he was five, he left a basin tap running with the plug in and flooded the bathroom.

8. He can make his ears waggle.

9. He has visited over a thousand schools.

10. He once scored minus ten in an exam! That's ten less than nothing!

11. His hair has gone grey, but his mind hasn't.

12. He'd like to have a pet tiger.

13. He'd like to learn the piano.

14. He has dreadful handwriting.

And a half . . . His favourite hobby is sleeping. He's very good at it.

This is the first story about my crazy family. We're not all crazy of course – it's Dad mostly. I mean, who would think of bringing home an alligator as a pet? It got into our next-door neighbour's garden and ate all the fish from his pond. It even got into his car! That gave him quite a surprise, I can tell you! He was not very happy about it. Mum says Crunchbag will have to go, but Dad and I quite like him, even if his teeth are rather big and sharp.

* * * * * * * * * * * * * * * * * * * *

Big problems in my family – we're running out of money fast. Dad reckons we should start up our own mini-farm. But the yoghurt we made exploded, and the goat needed an aromatherapy massage!

   That's the sort of daft thing that happens in my family. And then my baby bro, Cheese (yes – I know Cheese is a very odd name for a baby!), was spotted on national television showing off his bottom!